The Women's Press
science fiction

This is one of the first titles in a new science fiction series from The Women's Press.

The list will feature new titles by contemporary writers and reprints of classic works by well known authors. Our aim is to publish science fiction by women and about women; to present exciting and provocative feminist images of the future that will offer an alternative vision of science and technology, and challenge male domination of the science fiction tradition itself.

We hope that the series will encourage more women both to read and to write science fiction, and give the traditional science fiction readership a new and stimulating perspective.

JANE PALMER

Jane Palmer comes from a working-class background and describes herself as having been 'almost' educated. She has been employed in a variety of capacities: telephonist, ledger clerk, receptionist and milliner. She has 'managed to avoid' marriage and her beliefs are 'not many'. This is her first published book.

JANE PALMER

THE PLANET DWELLER

The Women's Press
sf

First published by The Women's Press Limited 1985
A member of the Namara Group
124 Shoreditch High Street, London E1 6JE

British Library Cataloguing in Publication Data

Palmer, Jane
  The planet dweller.
  I. Title
  823'.914[F]   PR6066.A44/

  ISBN 0-7043-3948-X

Typeset by MC Typeset, Chatham, Kent
Reproduced, printed and bound in Great Britain
by Hazell, Watson & Viney Ltd, Aylesbury, Bucks

Acknowledgement

I would like to acknowledge the assistance of astronomer Heather Couper, for whose advice on certain passages I am indebted.

1

'But hot flushes can be very embarrassing,' insisted Diana with a sincerity only the most stubborn of men could have doubted; unfortunately Dr Spalding was one of those men. However charming, sympathetic, attentive and good with children he might have been, his biology would never allow him the necessary comprehension of what Diana was talking about. Although he was stubborn, it was with a genuine concern for Diana's welfare that he assured her, 'But Hormone Replacement Therapy can have very unpleasant side-effects, my dear. I've heard of some women losing their finger-nails and others being stuck with headaches for weeks on end – and do you really want to go on having periods until you're past seventy?'

'I've already worn my finger-nails away by climbing up the wall and give my daughter regular headaches by screaming at every animate and inanimate thing that gets in my way,' Diana persisted. 'And will not live to be seventy if I carry on at this rate.'

'But in a short while these symptoms will be gone,' Spalding said soothingly. 'It would worry me to prescribe something I've never had dealings with before. Let me give you some more librium to tide you over.'

'They send me to sleep,' grunted Diana, knowing the quarry had managed to evade the net as he had done a dozen times before.

'At least it will give Julia the chance to relax,' he smiled, blissfully unaware that Diana was mentally digging his grave. 'Just take them as you need them, but don't overdo it. We don't

1

want you to get hooked, do we.' Diana managed to grimace a smile of false gratitude, and clutching the elegantly scrawled prescription strode sullenly home.

Only stopping to screw the prescription up with one hand and throw it in the pedal bin, she hauled her partially dressed daughter to the front door after her, and strode back outside on to the tarmac path.

'Didn't get it then, Mum?' Julia asked immediately, with an unusual understanding of the menopause for a child of eleven and a half.

'You won't find it so funny when you get to my age,' Diana promised her daughter with a marked lack of motherly affection.

'Oh, they would have thought of something much better by then,' Julia assured her with a practised indifference to her mother's intolerance. 'Besides, I haven't even started my periods yet. Can I have some money for crisps?' Without a word, Diana took out some of the silver she had hopefully put aside for the prescription she wanted and thrust it into her daughter's hand.

By the time they reached their different routes Julia's uniform was correctly arranged and buttoned, and Diana's mood mellowed enough for her to say, 'I'll be back at four, so don't go out to play until you've had some tea.'

'Well, will you give Yuri his magnifying glass back as you go past then?' Julia said, producing a flat box from her satchel. 'I promised to let him have it as I came home.'

'Oh, he wouldn't mind you dropping it in later. I can't see what he'd want it so urgently for.'

'It'd be better if I didn't take it to school with me. I'd hate to lose it.'

'Oh, all right. I have a few minutes to spare. Now don't be late, and I'll see you at teatime.'

'All right. Tarrah Mum,' and Julia trotted off after some of her friends.

As soon as they were out of sight, Diana made her way up the gravel path that led round the side of the terraced cottages towards the open-air museum of architecture where she worked. On the slope overlooking the meadow behind the cottages stood the less-well-maintained cottage belonging to Yuri. Having recovered enough of her natural tolerance, Diana braced herself to listen to Yuri's engaging babble for five minutes. Though totally harmless and likeable, his grasp of reality could seem a little crazy to a serious mentality, and Diana had a secret reason to wonder if she was becoming as crazy as him.

As she reached Yuri's isolated home, it crossed Diana's mind that he might be the only one she could confess the guilty secret to, but as soon as she walked into the garden that idea was immediately dashed. Yuri was lying quite drunk under his four-inch reflecting telescope with a fob-watch in one hand and a gin bottle in the other. A hard night's observation and excess of alcohol had undoubtedly affected his conversational ability for the next few hours.

Having ascertained that Yuri was still alive, Diana hauled him to his feet. Giving him the support his unsteady legs could not provide, she guided him into the cottage. There was not much of him, and she easily let him collapse on to an old horsechair sofa still clutching the fob-watch and the gin bottle.

Knowing from experience that Yuri would sleep solidly until the effect of the gin had worn off, then wake up to be his usual muddled self, Diana placed the magnifying glass on the table by a pile of exercise books filled with scribble. Fortunately it was midsummer, otherwise a heavy dampening dew might not have let Yuri off so lightly. Being not much less than fifty herself, Diana knew that as joints grew older they were fond of reminding their owners of their existence with more frequency. She covered the slumbering Yuri with a blanket and briefly watched his contented expression. Then she left, carefully closing the gate which was suspended on only one hinge.

The sun was obviously going to shine all day, so Diana left the carelessly discarded tarpaulin that protected the reflector hanging over the fence and made her way back on to the gravel path. She passed the reconstructed ancient buildings that sat like interlopers in the landscape. Many of them had never known cleaner or more pleasant surroundings, or even some of the parts that made them up. Most had been elegantly cobbled together from bits and pieces salvaged from demolition sites with the love and artistry of the dedicated. The brief glint of space-age technology above the trees as the sun's rays caught the edge of a smooth dish no longer seemed disconcerting to Diana, though it must have stopped many a lover of ancient architecture dead in their tracks. In less than fifteen minutes she was within sight of the timbered building that housed the museum offices.

By the time she had finished photocopying maps of ancient stone huts once lived in by stone-age people and wondering how many of them had lived to enjoy the menopause, Diana's desire to share her embarrassing secret had increased tenfold.

'Up to taking half a dozen kiddies round the iron-age farm, Di?' a voice sang out sweetly from the adjoining room of the partitioned Tudor hall.

In such an institution, a general secretary's duties could be as diverse as explaining to six-year-olds how to smelt metal and explaining to seventy-year-olds how much more hygienic their new council homes were compared with the picturesque hovels they had been moved from. So the question came as no great shock.

'The fresh air might agree with you,' the spectacled Mr Lowe told her, poking his head round the temporary wall.

Diana marvelled at the older man's concern for her health, though she was convinced he was not sure what made her break into trembling sweats and moods of uncontrolled irritation. Mrs Lowe had somehow managed to escape into her sixties with a graceful ease she envied.

'How far do they go?' Diana asked.

'Only as far as the dishes, they've got a teacher to take them round the rest,' Mr Lowe replied, relieved that she appeared to be in a moderately humane mood.

'All right,' she agreed, and left the photocopier for livelier company.

The teacher of the six junior-school pupils was wearing the same enthusiastically expectant look as her charges. Diana could tell they were anticipating wondrous revelations about the past from one who spent her life working next to it. Their guide was already entertaining as much knowledge about ageing as she wanted to know, however, and was unable to take a sympathetic view of times she was thankful were past. Diana had always been puzzled about more recent generations wishing themselves back into the unhygienic, monarchical and impoverished history of their ancestors. And it was with only the greatest difficulty that she could describe it as being anything other than that.

None of the children could imagine the shades of such poverty in those beautifully arranged and reconstructed buildings, though, and gawped at each in admiration and wonder. Those beautifully carved doorways and arches seemed to have been chiselled by inspired sculptors, not the bonded masons and carpenters who were ancestors to the builders of council houses. Despite all this, it was inevitable that when they reached the iron-age farm the attention of the group would be distracted. The massive metal dishes pointing skywards as they rumbled sedately down their tracks were more fascinating than primitive engineering.

Diana dutifully did her piece about how people lived so many hundreds of years ago, making it sound more like spring in Marie Antoinette's farm than midwinter in the frozen pig sty she felt it must have more closely resembled. Her romantic interpretation of the near unspeakable was lost on the young audience, however. They wanted to know what those huge tilted cereal bowls were doing.

'They're listening to the stars,' Diana explained, with the experience of someone who knew better than to use the word 'telescope' to describe them. But before any awkward questions beyond the limited scope of Diana or their teacher could be fired, deliverance was suddenly at hand.

'Mog! Mog!' screamed a figure running alongside the track waving its arms in a state of high agitation. 'Have you seen Bert

Wheeler? I'm going to kill him!'

With her open overall flapping round her legs and the hair escaping from her bun streaming about her face, the angry creature bounded up towards them with strides that should have been beyond her short legs.

'Hello, Eva,' smiled Diana sweetly. 'Just the person we wanted to see.'

'What for?' demanded Eva, suspecting Diana might be trying to divert her mind from murder.

'These children would like to know what those dishes are for.'

'Listening to the stars . . . and other things,' Eva explained automatically to the children who were already flinching at her arrival.

'And how do they listen to the stars, Eva?' Diana insisted.

'In the same way an optical telescope mirror collects light and reflects it to the eyepiece. These dishes reflect radio signals on to the dipole at the centre. With a computer we can combine the output from many dishes, which gives a better picture than if we used just one of them,' she went on, 'or at least we could if some idiot didn't keep opening up with a shotgun at any crows that look as though they're going to perch on them.'

'Oh . . . Bert Wheeler?'

'Bert Wheeler,' agreed Eva menacingly, and the teacher quickly made her farewells, fearful of having her pupils treated to the spectacle of this demented female and crow-shooting gentleman trying to beat each other to the draw.

'Of course,' Diana went on, when the tunics and felt hats had scuttled from sight through the cobbled courtyard of a market hall, 'he does think they are an invention of the Devil. His mother was the local witch and brought him up to believe that the only things to come from the stars were bad omens and lumps of rock.'

'The woman must have been an idiot.'

'You'd think a lump of rock that crashed through your greenhouse on a Sunday morning was a bad omen.'

At that, Eva's interest was suddenly aroused and she

demanded, 'A meteorite? Where is it now?'

'The old girl got her own back on it by telling Bert to take it down to Joseph to melt it down in his furnace. They smelted it and turned it into a cast-iron foot-scrape and a plaque to ward off the evil eye. Somebody got too vigorous with the foot-scrape, though, and it shattered.'

'The man's an idiot!' snapped Eva.

'I know,' agreed Diana. 'They should have worked it into wrought iron.'

'I mean – to melt the thing down in the first place. The man can't have any sense at all.'

'That's as may be, but there's not many who'll do his job for the pay.'

'You pay him to shoot at our telescopes, Mog? Your crowd are just as decadent and heathen as he is.'

'No we're not,' answered Diana, wishing she would for once call her by her right name. 'We just take things a little more sedately. After all, we're hardly paid anything like the wages you mob get.'

'There you go. On about money again. It's not my fault you wouldn't swot at school. We both had the same chance, you know.'

'I never said we didn't,' replied Diana, feeling her body tighten for one of her moods. 'It's just that you somehow managed to end up successful and prosperous and I ended up menopausal and broke.'

'Why don't you get something done about it? You've been like it for long enough.'

'Because Spalding is the only doctor in the area and I cannot afford private treatment.'

'Never mind,' sniffed the short untidy female from beneath a mop of hair that displayed every shade from grey to mouse. 'You'll always be better-looking than me. Always were, so I don't see why you shouldn't do some suffering for it. If you did manage to get HRT it'd only make you stay young, and you don't want that, do you?'

'Yes,' insisted Diana in a voice high-pitched in desperation.

7

'Just because it's impossible for you to look any more scruffy than you do now does not mean all women have the same rational acceptance of ageing that you've managed to work out in your logical mind.'

'So I'm a mess. If I had half your looks I would never have been taken seriously.'

'And apart from that . . .' Diana found herself blurting out.

'Go on.'

'I think I'm going mad.'

'Oh really . . . like violently, or like Yuri?'

'Like both,' was the taut reply.

Knowing at that point she would have been better off pursuing Bert Wheeler, something in the expression of her friend's hazel eyes riveted Eva to the spot. Her dotty companion did not become serious very often, even at the height of one of the moods she had been having for the past year. Instinctively Eva was on guard against saying the wrong thing. 'What's the problem then?'

'I hear a voice,' Diana confessed. 'It's as though someone keeps turning on a switch and transmitting something, then switching off again just as suddenly.'

'Told Spalding? You shouldn't be having problems of any sort after all this time.'

'I know,' was the flat reply. 'But I'm not imagining it. There really is a voice.' She could tell her friend's credence had been stretched beyond its non-elastic bounds.

Despite this, Eva still attempted to extend her belief a little longer. 'If there is, then it must be making some sort of sense?'

'It may be making sense to whoever owns the voice, but it doesn't to me. It only ever says one word, but I can still feel when it's there, though not speaking – as though it had left the transmitter open.'

'Where do you think it comes from then?' Eva's gaze slowly followed Diana's finger as it pointed heavenward. Convinced she knew as much about that direction as anyone could, Eva suddenly found herself shaking her head in disbelief.

'Why not?' demanded Diana.

'The human brain, in most cases, is a marvellous thing, but it does not have the receptivity of a radio telescope . . .' Eva faltered on the verge of an explanation.

'Perhaps you aren't pointing them in the right direction?'

'Now look, Mog,' said Eva firmly, 'I've had the same trouble with Yuri. We can't go swivelling the dishes about at the whim of someone who hears a voice from outer space. We have to work to a programme . . . and even if we could be sure you were receiving a signal from out there we would at least have to know that it was coming from more specific co-ordinates than the general direction of "up".'

'You don't believe me,' Diana protested.

'*You* obviously believe it. That will have to be enough. Though I've no doubt Yuri would find some sympathy with the condition if he could stop entertaining his own fantasies for five minutes.'

'There's no need to be so mean about him,' Diana cautioned her. 'He may not be right in the head, but we don't know what made him like that in the first place, do we?'

'It's a pity someone doesn't confiscate that reflector of his. I'm just thankful he busted the camera so he can't take any snaps of planets colliding.'

'It keeps him happy, and I'm sure he's not so stupid. He'd probably develop a permanent gin complex if he didn't have that telescope.'

'Him . . . no,' smiled Eva. 'He's already a perfect example of matter over mind. Do you know what he told me?'

'No. And I don't want you to tell me. If he does ever want to let me know anything I prefer him to tell me in his own way. I don't want you sneering to me about it before he does. Anyway, he does look after himself . . .' then, as an after-thought, remembering the state he had been in that morning, '. . . most of the while.'

Realising that her irrational friend was prepared to defend the crazy Yuri beyond the bounds of any reason she was liable to come up against, Eva asked innocently, 'What does the voice say then?'

Diana looked at her hard and long before replying, 'Moose-van.'

'Moo-se-van,' repeated Eva objectively. 'What's that?'

'What this voice keeps saying,' Diana said stubbornly, knowing she was wasting her breath in trying to convince Eva of anything.

'Nothing else?'

'Nothing else. Just "Moosevan".'

'Oh, good grief . . .' muttered Eva under her breath. 'Don't you think you should have some time off?'

'I am. Julia breaks up in a couple of days. No more parties of sticky little urchins coming down here and wanting to look through your radio telescopes for at least a week. Just think of that. You can hunt Bert Wheeler in peace, and roll those outsize ears up and down to your heart's content without needing to bother whether there are any bodies on the track. But if they do come across Moosevan in the process, just remember who heard it first.'

'Why don't you keep tuned in and let me know if it ever says anything else?' asked Eva mischievously. 'We'll let you have the credit if you discover something before we do.'

'Oh really . . .?'

'Why not?' shrugged Eva. 'There are some things radio astronomy shouldn't have to take the blame for,' and before she could say any more the report of a shotgun could be heard in the distance. 'Bert Wheeler!' she screeched with renewed vigour, and was off before Diana could say goodbye.

Strolling leisurely back to the Tudor hall, Diana felt the thankful mists of numbness creep over her recent memories of hot flushes and messages from outer space. A refreshing summer breeze brought back the recollection of the balmy, almost carefree, days of her long-lost youth and the bright-eyed smiling child the convention of those days would not let a sixteen-year-old unmarried mother keep. Eva was right about looks. She had managed to appear so dowdy the boys allowed her to continue her studies in peace. Diana had been the reverse and consequently was flattered into believing attraction was all, until she had the rewards of that attraction taken from her. From that time, caution had been her second name. Never to want marriage, but determined to have a replacement for her lost offspring. Just as she thought it was becoming too late, a man discovered that she was the girl of his dreams. Thinking a woman in her late thirties would be easy to hold, he slackened his grip in not insisting on marriage only to find his lady love and daughter had flown within a year. Diana should have felt guilty about the deception but all she could do was smile at the man's self-confidence.

'Come and meet the new temps,' sang out Mr Lowe as Diana entered the cool timbered hall. 'They're both from college so will need some local digs. Know of anyone who could put them up?'

Diana was about to recommend Flora and Irene who were sisters with a house larger than their prim activities needed when she set eyes on the students. Both looked as though they could not only have been happy to live in the iron-age farm, but blend in quite convincingly with its surroundings. One face was concealed by an outgrowth of beard unnatural on one so young and the other looked angelic enough for Diana not to be able to distinguish its gender.

'We're very lucky,' Mr Lowe babbled. 'They're both studying anthropology and know something about archaeology.'

Noting Diana's reluctance to say anything in haste, the bearded student mumbled something in an amiably low voice to which she managed to smile non-committally before she remembered something. 'Do you like farms?' she asked, at which Mr Lowe's eyebrows shot up towards his bald pate (he had obviously drawn the same conclusion about the iron-age village as she had) but they relaxed as she went on, 'One of our local farmers, Mr Cooper, has converted a stable to put up hikers. It has running water, and Mrs Cooper will cook if you don't mind eating with the farm-hands. If you like the idea I know she won't charge you much.'

As though she had just described a palace, the students' eyes lit up in enthusiasm and Diana sighed in relief that she had stopped herself from mentioning Irene and Flora in time. Although they had known her for years, they still insisted she should refer to herself as 'Mrs', as though illegitimacy was still a word not to be found in any dictionary. As they were coming to tea in a couple of days, guiding two inoffensive, but visually amazing, students to their doorstep might not have endeared her to them.

'What do I call you?' Diana suddenly thought to ask.

'My name's John,' announced the beard gravely.

'My name's Fran,' announced the other in a voice that still gave Diana no clue as to what gender its owner belonged to.

'I'm Diana. Most people call me Di.' She was about to add that that was because she often felt like death, but decided not to break up the amiable atmosphere. 'I hope you enjoy your stay here. If you're interested in astronomy I know one of the doctors at the observatory. I'm sure she wouldn't mind showing you around.' Although the heads nodded in gratitude, Diana could see the acute disinterest register in the eyes and she wondered how they would cope with the questions that were bound to be fired at them about the perambulating monsters at the bottom of their garden; not to mention the occasional enraged astronomer chasing Bert Wheeler whenever he had the urge to chase crows.

'Yes,' continued Diana, smiling inwardly at the thought of what delights awaited them, 'I'm sure you're going to enjoy yourselves here.'

'Sure . . .' murmured John shaking his head knowingly. 'This is our thing. Old places really appeal to us.'

'People too . . .' agreed Fran in a way that sent irritable prickles down Diana's back at the unintended faux pas.

'You won't mind showing John and Fran around, will you Di?' asked Mr Lowe. 'I'll have to finish these plans for the bridge before teatime.'

'Of course not,' smiled Diana as she choked back a bad taste in her mouth brought on by sudden nausea and the unwelcome awareness of ageing. 'I'll show them the way to Mr Cooper's afterwards if you like?'

'Marvellous idea,' agreed Mr Lowe. 'You can go straight home after that.'

Diana needed no second bidding. Seizing a handful of literature about the exhibits, she wasted no time in leading them to each one. John and Fran followed behind, laden with knapsacks like two obedient yaks. They drank in every word she uttered with rapt attention as they examined the reconstructed antique world they had such affinities with. Being more modern in outlook, Diana found their fascination baffling. She had genuine terrors of fires in thatched roofs and bats in belfries. Until meeting these two she had thought of her work as being little more than a matter of economics. Their reverent lulled tones echoing about the empty living-spaces made her feel quite guilty, and for the first time she actually found herself concentrating on the wonder of it all.

As she looked up with Fran and John into the silent timbers of a fourteenth-century barn, a faint familiar click sounded in the back of her mind. Gritting her teeth and clenching her fists she froze for fear of making some exclamation as the soft melodious voice broke into her thoughts.

'Moosevan,' it whispered. 'This is Moosevan . . .' then nothing for a few seconds before it seemed to fade with a sigh and distant click.

Fran and John must have taken her taut expression as being one of rapture and waited patiently while she reorganised her attention sufficiently to lead them on to the next exhibit. Although they hardly glimpsed the huge dishes gleaming in the sunlight, Diana found herself glaring at the nearest of them with an expression of suspicion and resentment at its smug indifference to her voice. When she was able to hear this creature so clearly it seemed an almighty waste of time and money that they between them could not. Half suspecting that the voice might have something to do with her condition, Diana was relieved to be able to return home early and have a good sulk for half an hour in the privacy of the bedroom she had papered and carpeted in peaceful pastel posies.

2

'No, no, not there,' the older voice of Julia bullied the small Chinese twins as they insisted on sitting next to each other and not in their allocated places around the fairy ring. 'If we go and leave gaps like that the giant can easily reach in and snatch one of us.'

Tom, with most of his face covered by a battered old top hat, warned, 'And he's got claws like a crab which will bite you in half,' thinking more of horror comics than fairies.

'We eat crabs,' Lin assured them with an expression that said his mind was more on his parents' cooking than the game in hand.

'I like your parents' food,' piped up the small voice of Vicky sitting opposite the twins. 'We're going to have sweet and sour pork on Friday with beanshoots and spring rolls and lotus root.'

'We picked mushrooms here this morning,' Kitty, Lin's twin, told her. 'There were at least fifteen around this ring.'

'Really?' asked Vicky wide-eyed in amazement. 'Did the fairies put them there?'

'Oh no. This ring is made by mushrooms growing under the ground,' said Kitty.

'Oh I do hate clever kids,' sneered Tom, who would rather it had been a magic barrier against the claw-fisted giant.

'We usually have dried mushrooms, but I like fresh ones much better,' Kitty added. 'Fairies may live here too.'

'If there are any giants about we'll be in a sticky mess if they don't,' Julia reminded them with the authority of the eldest.

'Mind you, it is a very big ring to try and surround, I suppose. Perhaps as long as we sit inside it they won't bother us.'

'I have never seen a fairy ring as big as this before,' said Vicky, lying on her stomach and trying to reach unsuccessfully across it. 'It is really huge.'

'I suppose there must be a fairy palace beneath it,' pondered Tom, taking off his top hat to lie flat and put his ear to the ground. 'It would only come up at night though. People would frighten them off.'

'What about Yuri and his telescope?' Kitty reminded him.

'Oh, Yuri wouldn't frighten anyone,' Vicky told her. 'The fairies probably like him.'

'Why don't you ask him if he's seen any?' Lin suggested.

'I'll do that when I go back,' Julia said. 'He called in to see Mum. I don't think he sees fairies though. He's always looking at the stars. He knows a lot about the stars and planets.'

'Oh yeah?' inquired Tom with his ear pressed to the soft grass.

'Did you know that apart from the big planets like Mars and Saturn, there are thousands and thousands of much smaller ones going round the sun as well?' Julia told them.

'Never,' sneered Tom.

'Well, there are. There must be because Yuri told me, and he can see them. They are so tiny he has to make this complicated map of where they are, then make another several hours later to see if they have moved. If they don't move then they are stars, if they do they're small planets.'

'Why?' asked Lin inoffensively in wide-eyed wonderment.

'Why?' echoed Julia. 'I don't know why, but he's got piles and piles of books full of writing and sums which tells him where they are.'

'Why bother to look at something so difficult to find?' Vicky giggled and joined Tom in pressing her ear to the ground.

'He must be very clever,' pondered Kitty and her twin shook his head in agreement.

'He must be,' added Lin, 'because he isn't like other adults.'

They were suddenly silenced by Vicky's shrill cry, 'I can hear them! Listen, listen,' and she pushed her ear closer to the ground.

'So can I, so can I!' whooped Tom, both of them unaware of Julia's disbelieving scowl.

Kitty and Lin were immediately down with their ears to the ground as well, and soon laughing at the sound they fancied they heard beneath it.

'Oh really . . .' sighed Julia, quite sure they were only doing it to try and get her to put her ear to the ground as well.

Their attention to the sound was too deep and sustained to be a practical joke though. Cautiously, Julia bent down and pressed her ear to the ground with them.

There was something down there. Too old to believe it could have been fairies like the other four, Julia felt an odd tingling on her scalp that told her there was something sinister about the low tuneful hum. The others listened in rapturous silence until it stopped as suddenly as it had started. Then they sprang up to join hands and dance in a tight circle around the mystified Julia and Tom's top hat.

'Oh, you are clumsy,' scolded Diana as she mopped the tea from Yuri's sweater. 'I've only just scrubbed Julia's experimental toffee off the kitchen floor. I don't want another mess on it. Why don't you hold the cup straight?'

'I do. I just have trouble getting it to my mouth,' protested Yuri. 'My hand will shake so much lately.'

'I'm not surprised. After the way I found you the other morning it's a wonder that's all that shakes.'

'But I only drink the gin to stop my hand shaking.' Yuri smiled so disarmingly Diana almost believed him.

'You shouldn't touch that stuff at all. How on earth do you manage to hold your telescope still?'

'Oh, I do not need to. The equatorial mounting makes it still or the motor will drive it.'

'Oh . . . Do you want another cup of tea?'

'No . . . no. I still have some left in this to spill.'

Diana rose to pour herself another cup and stood pondering

over the top of Yuri's head which was covered in crinkly grey curls that had somehow managed to grow outwards at different rates.

'Yuri . . .?' she said eventually.

'Yes?'

'I've been having a little trouble lately . . .'

'What sort of trouble?'

'I hear a voice in my head.'

Yuri was silent for a moment. 'That is very odd.'

'Haven't you ever heard voices in your head?' she inquired hopefully.

'Never,' he assured her. 'I talk to myself, but I never listen.' Then he added thoughtfully, 'But you should not hear voices. You are a healthy woman . . . as far as a woman your age can be healthy.'

'Thank you,' snarled Diana.

'I meant . . . because . . .' Yuri could not think of the right words, so she finished them for him. 'Because I am a menopausal female, hearing voices should be a quite natural pastime for me.'

'I didn't mean that.'

'Then what?'

'If you hear a voice, it is either because you are imagining it,' he could tell by her expression that that was out, 'or because there is someone talking to you.'

'How?'

'If there is someone talking to you from a great distance away, that means you are either telepathic,' Diana did not seem very enthusiastic about that and Yuri was relieved because he would not have believed it either, 'or that they have a transmitter and you have a receiver tuned in to their frequency.'

'My head?'

'If that is where you hear the voice, where else?' shrugged Yuri, not taking into account the reorganisation going on elsewhere in Diana's body. 'I would not say it is impossible, but telepathy is much more fashionable nowadays. Old-fashioned things like transmitters and receivers take the mystery out of unexplained messages.'

'I can do without those sort of mysteries, thank you; I prefer things I can understand through more conventional sources.'

'There is much money in being telepathic.'

'If I had to choose a dishonest way to make money I would sooner see fairies. Even if they aren't so fashionable.'

'Unfortunately one cannot choose the way to go mad. It is something which suddenly thrusts itself upon you.'

'You make that sound like the voice of experience. You can't really make up your mind whether you're crazy or not, can you?'

'If I could choose,' said Yuri intensely, 'then I would choose to be crazy.'

For a moment, Diana began to have doubts about his derangement, and not wishing any of his fantasies to ever prove themselves facts she ordered him, 'Come into the garden and see the roses.' Obediently, Yuri followed her through the French windows, quickly trying to swallow the rest of his tea and spilling it down his sweater. Diana did not comment as she saw him trying to brush it off with his sleeve, merely signalled him to remove it altogether. Again he obediently complied to reveal a striped sweater beneath it. Wondering whether his dress habits had been learnt in Siberia she pegged the tea-soaked sweater to the washing-line, watched it hang limply for a few seconds, then took it down again.

'I'll have to wash it,' she announced without a trace of apology.

'But I wash it last week. Why again?'

'It annoys me,' she declared in a voice that did not invite criticism. 'I am beginning to be annoyed by everything lately.'

'Have you seen Dr Spalding?' asked Yuri innocently, sensing that her glance could have struck him dead for thinking of the question.

'I have seen Dr Spalding too often to do my temper or health any good.'

'Oh . . .' he mused. 'He give me tranquillizers as well.'

'What did you see him for?'

'I was taken to him when I have this accident.'

'What accident?'

'I stop some shot . . .' he murmured.

'You were shot!' shrieked Diana. 'How on earth did you manage to get shot?'

'I think he aimed for the crow, but that flew away,' Yuri briefly explained and made to escape to the other end of the garden.

'Bert Wheeler,' groaned Diana. 'And what were you doing near those telescopes? Eva must have gone mad.'

'She did not know. Bert said he was very sorry and we agree to say nothing. I was doing nothing with her stupid radio telescopes. What could I have been up to?'

'Whatever it was, getting shot must have made a good second. So why did Spalding prescribe tranquillizers for gunshot wounds?'

'It was just a graze. I just take them to humour him. He is a good man really.'

'Just bloody incompetent. And I want you to promise me . . .'

Yuri raised his hands in surrender and promised never to go near Dr Eva Hopkirk's precious toys again.

'Or Bert Wheeler,' added Diana. 'Why go there anyway?'

'I like looking at those expensive toys. They remind me of . . .' His words trailed off and Diana could tell by the distant look in his eyes she should not demand to know what he was thinking of. Yuri wandered to the bottom of the garden and watched the children in the meadow with their ears to the ground in the middle of the fairy ring. With his back to her, Diana was not able to see the suddenly tense expression cross his usually relaxed face. He stood there for some minutes until they all sat up and the four youngest began to dance in a circle. By the time he turned away from the happy gathering Diana was hanging his dripping sweater on the line.

'That was quick,' he commented.

'I had some stuff in soak and used that water. I'm not sure it would stand up to a spinning with the rest, though the washing will have to go out before the others arrive,' Diana told him.

'Others?'

'Irene, Flora and Daphne,' announced Diana, blocking his way to the gate before he could bolt. 'And there's no need to go because of them.'

'I have some calculations to do.'

'Rubbish.'

'That Mrs Daphne Trotter woman hates me,' pleaded Yuri. 'I know she does not want to see me.'

'Just because she shouts abuse at you about the state of your garden every time she rides past does not mean she hates you. It's just that the English have firm ideas about keeping gardens tidy.'

'And that horse knocks gate off its hinge. It hates me as well. I always like horses, but this one hates me. They are both bullies.'

'The woman's a little eccentric, that's all,' Diana tried to pacify him.

'The world was conquered by these harmless English eccentrics. The rest of the world and me do not think them harmless.'

'Look . . . I'll make sure she doesn't start on you. But I have to invite her if I invite Irene and Flora or they'll think I'm snubbing her.'

'Why not? It is a good idea. I suppose I will have to tidy up for this Mrs Precious woman?'

'Well, you do look a right little scruff,' Diana reminded him. Finding no grounds for disagreement, he replied, 'I like being a scruff. I will not tidy up for Mrs Daphne. You make me stay, I will stay like this.'

'All right. It's difficult to see what can be done about it now.'

'You wash my best sweater so it is your fault.'

'Well, can't you just roll your sleeves up to hide the holes in the elbows?'

'All right. But I will not comb my hair.'

'I wouldn't know the difference if you did,' Diana muttered before walking into the kitchen to pull the clothes from the sink and throw them into the spin-drier. Yuri rolled the sleeves of his sweater up to hide the holes in them and reveal the holes he had in the sleeves of his shirt underneath that, and with much fiddling and adjusting managed to reach the happy balance where he was able to conceal both. Ignoring the grimace that Diana made at his hardly improved appearance, he put the dirty cups into the sink she had just emptied. Knowing the expected guests would be treated to the best tea service he put the teapot in as well and vigorously turned the tap on to flush the tealeaves away, only to splash them all over the front of his striped sweater. After pondering on what he could be expected to do about that for a few seconds, he turned to see Diana rummaging about in the pedal bin for the librium prescription she had thrown away two days ago.

'Damn!' she snapped as she realised the dustman had it. 'Damn! Damn! Damn!' Then, to make matters worse, the doorbell rang. 'Don't move,' she ordered Yuri, and dashed to answer it.

Yuri could hear the fond greetings echoing down the narrow hall and the boots of Mrs Daphne clip clopping after the others on the polished floorboards. In his mortal terror he fancied he could hear her spurs rattle as well and, not daring to look round to make sure she had gone into the living-room, was suddenly startled by her overbearing form standing in the kitchen doorway.

Her tight lips uttered not a word as she viewed the tea-stained Yuri, the washing part-hauled from the drier and the contents of the pedal bin scattered over the floor. The gleam of the hunter spying the fox crept into her cold eyes before Diana's voice could be heard from the other room.

'In here Daphne, I haven't finished tidying up out there yet.'

This made the cruel lips twist into a smile before their owner turned with a slap of the thigh and creak of boot leather to join the others. Yuri half expected a pack of hounds to come bounding up the hall after her. He nervously brushed the tealeaves from his sweater in readiness to make his escape through the front door should they not materialise, but Diana came shooting in before he could.

'I'll make the tea, Yuri. You can keep the girls entertained. Take that sweater off, you've got a reasonably good shirt on underneath it.' He obeyed and she saw the holes in the shirt, 'Well, at least it's clean.'

'I am not going near that Mrs Daphne Trotter. I never realise how good she make the horse look till now.'

'I'll only be a couple of minutes,' pleaded Diana. 'They'll troop out here if you don't.'

With a grimace of disapproval and irritably plucking at the badly tied scarf round his neck, Yuri bowed to her wishes and ambled into the living-room where Irene immediately greeted him with, 'Why hello Yuri, I haven't seen you for ages.'

'You are all right aren't you?' twittered Flora in her bird-like fashion. 'We heard you had an accident.'

'Accident?' murmured Yuri in innocent amazement. 'What sort of accident should I have?'

'Oh, weren't you shot after all then?' sneered Daphne with all the charm of a scavenging shark. Yuri burned to know how she had found out about him being shot, but was determined she should not have the satisfaction of making him admit it.

'No . . .' he smiled calmly, 'I was nearly stamped on by horse though.'

Having no sense of humour, Daphne chose to ignore his snipe at her equine pursuits and sang out with an accent that could have cut glass, 'You shouldn't drink so much and lie in the grass then, dear boy.'

'Oh really . . .' blushed Flora, knowing quite well about Yuri's fondness for a drink, but too much of a lady to put that knowledge into words. 'We mustn't embarrass Yuri like that, Daphne.'

'You will make him think the English are terrible people,' Irene agreed with her sister, they probably being the only local people soft enough to tolerate the friendship of the bossy Daphne Trotter.

'Beats me where he manages to find the money for drink,' Daphne went on. 'It wouldn't surprise me if the Russians gave him a pension to stay in this country.' Catching the gist of the last comment as she was about to enter, Diana's foot struck the living-room door with such force that its resulting crash against the sideboard made even the steel-spined Daphne jump.

'Tea!' she announced, more by way of a threat than an invitation, and Flora and Irene instantly breathed a sigh of relief.

'Have you discovered any more of those little planets?' Flora asked Yuri.

'I do not think so. They already have been discovered by someone before I see them. I only look for alignments.'

For some reason, Diana sensed something guarded in Yuri's manner and when Daphne decided to chip in on the conversation, she knew she would have to wait before she could prise anything more from him. 'What d'you mean? They're making patterns in the sky or something?'

'Something like that . . .'

'What rubbish,' she snorted. 'What makes you think that?'

'I have a good telescope.'

'All right then. So what does it mean?'

'Well . . .' Yuri began ponderously. 'Now, you know everything revolves around the sun because of its gravitational attraction?' The blank faces showed no signs of opposition to that Newtonian principle. 'Well, when different planets are lined up this gravitation increases more and more. Until eventually, when all the planets are lined up together, the gravitational attraction will be so great they will fall into the sun one by one.'

Not realising he was mocking them, Irene and Flora sat listening to him in wide-eyed innocence with the conviction that he was talking about somebody else's solar system. Daphne darted him a sideways glance that told him she thought he should have been locked up long ago. Diana took the coward's way out and asked sweetly, 'Biscuit anyone?'

Managing to keep Yuri there until Flora, Irene and Daphne had left, Diana remembered his statement about the planetoid alignments and was curious to discover if this could have been the story he had told Eva.

'What have you found out about the asteroids then, Yuri?' Diana asked, coming straight to the point, but he was reluctant to answer. 'I did tell you about my voice.'

'I told Dr Eva and she laughed,' he said. 'And she should know what I was talking about. They are only interested in listening to scintars and pulsars on the other side of infinity. These lumps of local debris are too close for them to waste time on, and if they are not interested what chance would there be of you believing me?'

'I'm not Eva, am I, Yuri,' Diana said, sitting beside him on the settee. 'Would it be so terrible to share the secret with me as well?'

'Of course not, Diana. You promise not to think me mad though?'

'Of course not,' lied Diana.

'Because if you don't believe me, then I will think I'm mad to see such things. I have been watching the planetoids for many years. Long ago I discovered that some of these small planets briefly formed patterns. I put it down to coincidence, but the more I study them, the more I become convinced that these patterns are not natural even though they have orbits more eccentric than I am. It is as though something is turning and guiding them to take different positions in the sky without interrupting their trajectories.'

'But surely somebody else must have noticed this. You can't be the only one looking at the asteroid belt.'

'Of course not. But each planetoid is so small that it is difficult to find one or two at a time, even with photographs. It does not occur to many to make out their positions in relation to each other mathematically over long periods of time.'

'This is what you have been doing?' asked Diana.

'For many years,' he said. 'And the more I learn, the more I am convinced that these little bodies are forming themselves into symmetrical groupings from which they will be able to draw together like a gigantic jigsaw puzzle.'

Although she desperately did not want to believe what Yuri

was telling her, for some reason, his conviction was impressive.

'I do not want this to be true,' Yuri explained after she had been silent for some while. 'But how can I disbelieve the findings of my own eyes?'

'Would it matter very much if they did come together and form another planet?' she asked thoughtfully.

'Not as things are now, because their mass would only make a very small body which would not affect our position in space. If that were the only thing . . .'

'What else?'

'Just in case you do believe me, I dare not tell you,' whispered Yuri. 'It would be too worrying to you to think about. Just keep calling me crazy so I eventually have to believe you and not worry about it myself.'

'You are a strange one. What happened to make you like this?'

'Nothing that terrible perhaps. It isn't always unreason that addles the brain.'

'Will you promise me something?'

'What is it?' he said, already half suspecting.

'No more gin . . . or whisky . . . or any alchohol,' was the demand. 'I wouldn't put it past Daphne and her gallant steed to trample all over you if they did find you lying drunk in the grass.' Yuri laughed silently at that. 'She is a wicked woman. You know that better than I do, but she's got powerful enough connections not to need to worry about being disliked. What their family never inherited they bought up.'

'Do not worry, Diana,' Yuri told her, 'I have a good friend and powerful woman on my side as well.' Diana was flattered by the description, even though she was far from seeing herself as a powerful woman.

3

'If the ancient races were so advanced they would not have left us with the prospect of slow extinction,' growled the representative of the most dangerous species in the dwindling galaxy. 'My empire proposes to the other races here that we colonise what fertile planets are left. It is hardly fair that one planet creature should be able to keep a world all to itself.'

Murmurs of approval from the tame audience ascended to greet the Mott's huge ears. They so flattered his oratory that for a brief second he actually wondered what democracy could be like. That concept had disappeared with the old races though, and only rumours of what it involved remained.

The dull green sun loured down unromantically on the clusters of high-ranking dignitaries from every part of the wispy barred galaxy. As the sun sank rapidly below the horizon, they could see the bleakness of their isolation in the distant pitch-black sky. Beyond the disorganised collection of blasted supernova remnants and small dense stars lay nothing. Not so much as a gas cloud or remote galaxy. Their part of the universe had indeed appeared to go out like so many pinpricks of light retreating into infinity.

With the stars had fled the old civilisations. They had been so advanced that the ones left behind had never been able to make contact with them when they were there, let alone understand what they said. Not being able to plead with the Old Ones to save them as well, the more recent civilisations were deserted like a floundering ship in a time-extinguishing whirlpool. Their suns had made nearly one circuit of their galaxy since then, but traditions of those ancient people's benevolence still echoed from recordings. Lately though, as the habitable planets disappeared through natural ageing and the warlike policies of the Mott, most species had begun to wonder just how charitable the Old Ones had been to have left them in such a predicament. The Mott were aggressive, not particularly bright, and so committed to building their empire that the races not represented at the gathering were the races they had extinguished. But who else could the survivors turn to? Even the Torrans, reputedly the most intelligent species, had managed to disappear en masse. Compared with the other races, they were believed to be too delicate to survive anyway.

There was little to recommend detailed description of many members of the gathering. Most of them at some time or other had resorted to genetic engineering to preserve themselves from extinction, and their efforts had produced far less pleasing results than Nature's. She had been relegated to trimming whatever fringes of the galaxy the Mott had so far not found any use for. Needless to say, there were many greys, dingy greens and several shades of puce rubbing fin with scale that night.

Apart from the judderingly abrupt sunset and ascent of the artificial green moon, the other entertainment came from a slimy chorus who had managed to ease themselves from their shells for the occasion. Eventually, even the Mott representative came as a welcome relief from their painfully drawn-out dirge in memory of some obscure warrior.

'As we are in agreement, we must work out a course of action,' he told them. 'The Mott will act as co-ordinators.'

'But what about the Jaulta Code?' piped up a thin voice from the audience, and its owner was immediately admonished by the Mott.

'What about the Code? For thousands of years we have been trying to decipher it. Why should we be successful now? It was left by the old races to keep us hoping, not because it would show us how to escape this galaxy if we deciphered it. The only ones who can save us now are ourselves. We will take what we have a right to. These planet dwellers are not like us. They live at our expense.'

Again a rumble of approval rippled through the crowd and drowned any more thin piping voices that might have tried to make constructive comments. Eventually, when their meeting on the subject of self-preservation at any cost came to an end, agreement about how to tackle their expansion in a dwindling galaxy had been arrived at. It was naturally decided to drive out the creatures who inhabited the planets they wished to expand to. Far easier than training clever people to sit, or stoop – depending on their anatomies – for the best part of their lives in trying to translate the impossible Jaulta Code. Even if it did convey some solution to their slowly encroaching predicament, violence would undoubtedly prove much quicker.

Far in the depths of a well-furnished bunker that protected its occupants from the radiation of their own failed experiments, three creatures sat viewing each other with stern green expressions of disapproval. An onlooker might have been excused for thinking they did not like each other, but it was in the nature of their particular species, the Olmuke, to like nothing, not even themselves. Self-dislike being the most potent motivator, next to fear, for engineering the despicable, these three had the highest qualifications for carrying out the work of assassinating a planet.

Before them stood the three-dimensional map of their first quarry. It was a pale, lush world without any great oceans, but enough water to keep the vegetation abundant and banks of cloud to disperse it. It revolved at a comfortable distance around a stable yellow sun, and would only need slight adjustments in its atmosphere to ideally suit the Mott. As these were the wealthiest, and consequently the most powerful and dangerous species, they were to be first in receiving the fruits of the green trio's endeavours.

Jannu flicked the image off with the middle toe of his splayed foot. He leant back to rub the top of his flat head with a six-fingered nailless hand. 'If this one goes right, we shouldn't have much trouble with the others,' he announced.

'If this one does not go right, we'll have quite a bit of trouble with the Mott,' Kulp reminded his partner in crime. 'I have this peculiar attachment to my own skin and am determined nothing will go wrong.'

As neither of the others was likely to be as attached to Kulp's skin as he was, Tolt said, '*Your* space-distort net, remember. *You* can take the blame if it doesn't work.'

'I take the reward if it does,' Kulp snarled.

'We take twenty per cent each,' the others promptly reminded him, unwilling to be brow-beaten by the arrogant engineer. After all, *they* had provided space freighters for the expedition and had raised the battalion of robots to transport the beacons for the net.

'Have you noticed that if the Mott occupy this planet they will have completed a series of stations around the most densely populated clusters?' asked Jannu.

'So?' sniffed Kulp. 'We'll be their friends.'

'It can't have escaped the attention of some other politicians,' mused Tolt. He glanced accusingly at Kulp. 'Least of all someone with your massive intellect.'

'I am a pragmatist,' Kulp explained without apology. 'Our own species did not appreciate my talent, but the Mott do. If it so happens that I land on the winning side, it will be because they recognised my potential.'

'Well . . .' said Tolt, 'what you were putting your talent to on our planet would hardly have endeared anyone to you.'

'Are you complaining?'

'Not yet. But I might reserve that right.'

'You're in too deep to have rights,' Kulp reminded them. 'Squirming like hooked sea serpents when things start getting tough won't help you. Besides . . . what is there to worry about? What sort of opposition can we expect from the planet? These creatures have always been pacifists. They wouldn't even let anyone fight on their behalf.'

'I wonder why . . .' murmured Jannu thoughtfully. 'There is something definitely unnatural about that.'

'Just because most of the galaxy are warriors does not mean there cannot be exceptions,' laughed Tolt in a guttural splutter. 'What's the point in having so many warriors if there aren't a few victims?'

'Aren't we advanced . . .' sneered Jannu with even more self-disgust than the others had. 'I wonder if this is really progress?'

'Why worry?' shrugged Kulp. 'It's now that matters. Now and how much you can make out of it. So let's survey the system for any possible distort factors.'

In a room below the chamber where they had sat, the three-dimensional image of the planet they had been watching was projected into a large sphere. Smaller and smaller the planet became until the complete solar system and sun was revolving before them in reduced splendour. Running a grid over each section of the projection, Kulp carefully checked out every flaw, comet and piece of space debris that inhabited the system, until eventually he came to a justification for their search. He flicked the grid on and off once or twice as though not believing its findings.

'What's the matter?' Jannu demanded.

Kulp did not reply. He left the grid encircling the planet, and operated a cone-shaped measure which could pick out and localise the smallest space distortion. This obviously brought him to the same conclusion as the grid, and having satisfied himself, Kulp rocked back on his heels to announce, 'There's a compressed black cavity circling that planet.'

'Can't be,' Tolt immediately protested, though he knew Kulp would never have made such a statement had he not been sure.

Kulp's ego would never let him make mistakes, and he insisted, 'It's causing a space distortion equivalent to a small collapsar.'

'But the planet would have been torn apart by now if that was so,' protested Jannu.

'Nevertheless . . .' Kulp pondered, 'it obviously hasn't been, so we must assume either that it is artificial, or that the planet has some control over it.'

'Will it affect the space-distort net?' asked Tolt.

'Not when I've finished adjusting it. If it doesn't act on the planet, I'm pretty sure I can do something to prevent it counteracting the net.'

If any of them had had any intuition in place of their limitless confidence they might have stopped to wonder what had caused their quarry's unlikely companion, sinister in both presence and motion. It defied every law of physics Kulp knew, but his logical mind told him that as it was there it would have to be dealt with. Just because someone or something had managed to place it there without it sucking in the surrounding solar systems, did not mean they were more superintelligent than he was. The mathematics which held it inert could probably be unravelled with time, but Kulp decided to simply isolate it from interfering with his distorting net.

Once on board the service freighter, Tolt activated the jolt of power that unkindly woke from a dreamless lethargy the thousand robots who were to carry potentially explosive beacons.

'Work, you idle junk piles,' he muttered, feeding the first of Kulp's renewed instructions through their obedient circuits.

As the beacons had to be adjusted, and the distorting net these would create redesigned to surround the collapsar, the Mott's budget for the exercise would have to be doubled. Kulp was more concerned about the technique he was creating for wringing the planet creature from its cosy shell. But the Mott did have the reputation of being the touchiest species ever to bumble part way up the evolutionary spiral, and, above all, they were touchiest about parting with their wealth.

With the beacons adjusted, the robots were put to sleep until they were needed again. As they had so many automated servants to crew the space vehicles, Kulp, Jannu and Tolt were able to have a ship each to themselves, which suited their inborn anti-social natures a treat. Especially Kulp, who could be almost paranoid about letting any inferior being even touch his preciously expensive ship. He regarded it with the nearest thing to affection an Olmuke could have for anything.

Although Jannu and Tolt occasionally spoke ship-to-ship on their tedious journey, Kulp was left alone. By the time they met up with the Mott monitoring station, Kulp had completed the mathematics of his web of compensations, so it was with his usual arrogant step that he strode into the commander's observation chamber.

'We had to compensate for a black distort cavity, but everything is ready,' he announced to the Mott's back without introduction or apology, knowing the Mott would not understand the mathematics sufficiently to be able to contradict him.

The cascade of black ringlets matted together at their ends to join the Mott commander's belt did not give any indication their owner was alive let alone had heard what Kulp said. Kulp knew the species well enough and stood in silence to wait for the acknowledgement of someone who rivalled him in arrogance. Slowly the Mott turned to reveal his slit eye and trio of tusks. Having four wide short legs and an equally short pair of arms with immensely long fingers, Jannu and Tolt could not help wondering if evolution had quite finished designing the species when the genetic engineers took over. The commander switched his translator on and indicated Kulp should repeat his message. Kulp switched his translator on and obliged, as though the Mott should have understood it the first time.

Not comprehending the best part of what Kulp explained in a deliberately confusing way, the Mott decided not to show his ignorance of the figures. He could feed them through a machine which would explain them for him later. Instead he feigned the thoughtfulness of an intellectual as most tyrants do at some time or other to justify their actions. He hoped this might confuse his green visitors just as Kulp had succeeded in confusing him with his sums.

'I have been pondering on the fragile state of our galaxy, my friends,' the Mott explained, as though they would be profoundly interested in his findings, while knowing that all three of them would have felt more at ease with any one of the polished robots operating the station. 'I have been wondering how the older species managed to construct the ships to take them from this galaxy. There were no other galaxies within range then either and such a distance must have been impossible even for them.'

'It isn't recorded anywhere,' Kulp said. 'Perhaps they didn't make it. Whatever they were and how many, we can only guess, but it seems probable to me that we were the ones to survive and they died somewhere on the edge of the universe.'

'That's what I thought!' snapped the Mott in irritation.

It had been difficult for the Mott to accept that the rest of the galaxy did not love their empire-building species, especially as they had bestowed such benefits as advice and bombs in exchange for their freedom, but to have to listen to someone of greater genius was more than they could bear. And who were these green, flat-headed creatures anyway? Then he thought of the space-distort net and his temper sweetened. 'Many, many theories have been formed about the subject by those time-wasting thinkers my people are always trying to dispose of, but I doubt if the solution to it matters as much as they would have us believe.'

'I understand the Olmuke have discouraged such activities as well,' Kulp agreed, 'though I have not been back to confirm this for myself recently.'

'Of course not,' sneered the Mott. 'One could hardly expect you to.'

'However the older species managed to escape must be considered irrelevant,' Kulp went on. 'Let us just be thankful they did not decide to stay and make the galaxy more crowded than it is.'

'And their strange ideas about fairness and justice might have cramped our styles if the records are to be believed,' sniggered the Mott through his wickedly curved tusks. 'What freedom would they have left us to operate in?'

'I doubt that they would have even left us alive. I sometimes think those rebellious Torrans understand more about the old species than they are willing to admit and are trying to resurrect their old-fashioned ideas. The way they disappeared means they must be up to something.'

'They'll never get far, they'll never get far. They don't have the strength to cause much trouble. They're pretty ineffectual creatures when it comes to fighting.'

'Must be the only ones who are,' Tolt observed, from what he thought to be the safety of the far side of the chamber, but he was mistaken to think he was out of the Mott's translator's range since that specimen snapped, 'And where would you be without our wars and victories, my green-featured friend? Probably running some physical exercise group on your insignificant little world with all the other defeatists secretly dreaming of becoming warriors.'

Tolt said nothing because he knew he could never win the argument and Kulp said nothing because he agreed with the Mott. Jannu had long since lost interest in the conversation and was trying to engage a promising-looking robot in discussion. Noting the lack of response to his challenge about the insignificance of their planet, the Mott grunted in disgust, 'You green things are all spineless.'

'As long as we are paid we'll be almost anything your ego needs,' promised Kulp insincerely, and the Mott could not avoid noticing that wealth was a matter Kulp took as seriously as his own species.

'You'll be paid, you'll be paid, friend Kulp. You make sure we have that planet in the time we specified and you'll be paid in full.'

'I will complete my side of the bargain, Commander. Be assured that Moosevan will die.'

4

'I've found a mushroom! I've found a mushroom!' Vicky
squeaked in her thin voice as she danced round the outside of
the fairy ring clutching her treasure.

'Let me see,' ordered Julia. 'Don't eat it,' she added quickly.

'Why not?'

'Because horses come through this field,' Julia reminded her
as she saw Mrs Trotter and her black beast in the distance.

'Oh, all right.' Vicky carefully put it in her pocket with the
old pine cone and flint shaped like an arrow head. Then Kitty
held out a blue and yellow marble and waved it tantalisingly in
the air before her. Without hesitation, Vicky surrendered the
mushroom in exchange for the marble and Kitty popped the
delicacy in her mouth and swallowed it before Julia was able to
call out, 'Oh honestly . . . that could have had all sorts of dirt
on it.'

'It was clean,' protested Vicky at the accusation that she
could have poisoned her best friend. 'Mrs Trotter never comes
down this far. She always goes past Yuri's gate.' Sure enough,
Daphne Trotter and her hooved friend seemed to be about to
pay the unfortunate astronomer a visit.

If Yuri had heard Daphne's unusually silent approach he
would have stopped polishing the frame of his reflector and
beaten a hasty retreat, but the first thing he knew about it was
her cutting tones calling out, 'I suppose that must be the only
thing you bother polishing?'

Knowing it was too late to dash inside and pretend he had not seen or heard her, Yuri's dignity would only allow him to reply unenthusiastically, 'Good afternoon Mrs Trotter,' and then he carried on carefully rubbing his most precious possession.

Daphne was hardly going to be put off by the disgruntled tone in his voice, though. 'I see you haven't done much about your garden yet?'

'Why deprive the field voles and mice of a home?' asked Yuri. 'I like things the way they are.'

'You know that cottage is under lease to whoever you rent it from, don't you?' She leant over the side of her huge black mount to peer threateningly down at him.

'I have heard . . .' muttered Yuri carefully.

'And I've discovered that one of the conditions of that lease is proper maintenance of the property by the resident,' she informed him with relish, but he just shrugged his shoulders. 'You don't even know who leases this land do you, my little Russian misfit?'

'I know it is not you, Mrs Trotter,' Yuri said firmly, not seeing how she could counter that.

'Not yet,' she replied with the fixed smile of a crocodile, and the duster fell from Yuri's hand at the horror of what she was insinuating. 'Don't look so crestfallen, Yuri. I'm sure you must have another home somewhere behind the Iron Curtain.'

'I cannot go back there,' he tried to explain, though he knew such appeals to her better nature would be exhausted before they found it. 'Why hate me so much?'

'I don't hate you, Yuri,' explained Daphne with the peculiar conviction of the hypocrite, 'but I believe everyone has a place on this earth . . . and yours isn't here. Your people are a threat to the peace of the world and I don't see why one of them should have the benefit of the protection of this country.'

'But I and my people have little to do with what policies our leaders pursue.'

'Then that is their look-out. You can find somewhere else to set up home if you like, but by the time I've finished there'll be no aliens in this village.'

At that, pictures rose in his mind of Daphne Trotter riding

out of the village the family who owned the Chinese take-away, Mr Singh the dentist and himself. She would even probably have galloped down to Mr Cooper's farm and set about the two anthropology students had she known they were staying there.

'And don't go running to Diana, she can't help you. She's got problems of her own to worry about,' warned Daphne. 'I'll see you again tonight when I have the lease to the property, then I've no doubt I'll soon be able to find a young local couple who won't be too idle to do some gardening,' and with a click of her tongue and prod of her heels into the horse's flanks she left the stunned Yuri looking helplessly after her and wondering if she had not invented it all to frighten him.

With little enthusiasm he picked up the duster to carefully buff the frame of the telescope, muttering, 'Oh, Mr and Mrs Trotter, why did you decide to have that little girl? She is not healthy in head.'

The children in the fairy ring watched Daphne gallop off and wondered what they had been talking about.

'I think she was asking to have a look through his telescope,' Lin suggested.

'Oh, she was probably nagging him about his garden again,' Julia told them, well aware of what sort of woman Daphne was. Diana was unable to keep her opinion of the creature to herself once one of her moods came over her. 'She always is. But Yuri says he likes to keep it like that for all the wild animals to live in. I saw this tiny dormouse up there the other day, and a baby fox.'

'They were probably hiding from Mrs Trotter,' Tom remarked gravely. 'They were hunting foxes the other Sunday.'

'I think that's very cruel,' said Vicky wrinkling up her nose. 'They teach us to be kind to animals at school, but one of our teachers goes out hunting as well!'

'That hairy student called John who works at the museum told me that he belonged to a group who go around upsetting people who hunt foxes,' Julia explained. 'He and his friend put some aniseed down to confuse the hounds and the other Sunday Mrs Trotter got very upset. They say she still is.'

'Why would she still be so upset about that?' asked Kitty innocently.

'Well . . . I don't think it was that so much as the fact that on the way back her horse went and tipped her into the stinging nettles at the bottom of Yuri's garden. She was stung terribly badly.'

'The fairies should have kissed her better,' Vicky said thoughtfully.

'If you were a fairy, would you have kissed her better?' Tom asked.

'I would have though it was more a job for the goblins,' added Julia.

'That was probably what she was telling Yuri off about,' Vicky deduced.

'Serves her right for killing little foxes,' said Lin. 'I wouldn't like her to come and kill our little puppy.'

'Oh, that's not likely to happen,' Julia reassured him. 'Your mother said that when it grows up it is going to be a very big dog. It will probably be able to eat one of her hounds.'

At that, Tom and Kitty began crawling about the ring on all fours snarling and snapping at each other.

'You'll wake the fairies up doing that,' Julia said.

'Shall we listen to see if they are talking again?' suggested Vicky.

After what she had heard the other day, Julia was not that keen. She had felt too foolish to mention it to her mother, but worried enough to wonder what could have caused the humming sound. 'Perhaps they don't like us eavesdropping,' she warned Vicky. 'They might even get angry if they knew we were here.'

'Let's all hold hands and ask them to come up to us,' Vicky suggested.

'All right,' agreed Julia, and she drove the two dog imitations from the centre of the circle and told them to sit up and hold hands.

Yuri had lost interest in cleaning his reflector and stood idly, leaning over his partially suspended gate looking down the slope to where the children were playing. There was something apprehensive in his expression brought on by more than the visit of the local bully.

'Fairy, fairy, come and play . . .' he could hear the children cry. Then they stood up to join hands and stomped inelegantly round inside the fairy ring, swinging their arms in time to the repetitive chant. Yuri started slowly down the meadow towards them, as if every step they took increased some terror he had been nursing for years. He was about to raise his hand to warn them not to make so much noise when the grass in the centre of the fairy ring gently began to ripple apart. The children noticed this as well and immediately stopped their game. Although they had been calling on the fairies to come and play, they had hardly expected the invitation to be taken up. Julia quickly snatched the younger ones out of the circle and stood rooted to the spot in hypnotised fascination.

Being much younger, the others were far from terrified as a transparent shape full of squares, diamonds and circles materialised in the centre of the ring. It twinkled and sparkled at them like fairy treasure as though inviting them to come into its world. Kitty was so fascinated she took a faltering step forward to touch it, only to be warned back by Yuri's emphatic, 'No! You must not move!'

'What is it, Yuri?' asked Julia in fright, as the web of different shapes turned and twisted up and down in a spiral fashion.

'It is a sort of strobe effect,' Yuri tried to explain, just as alarmed as she was. 'It is being projected from the ground, and though you cannot see it, those shapes are really moving very fast. If you were to touch one of them it might cut your fingers off.'

'But if it's only a projection, my hand should go straight through it.'

'Not with this projection. It is linked to something far above us.'

'But how, Yuri, how?'

'I cannot explain easily, Julia, but it will soon go,' he replied, hoping that he was right.

It did not fade though, if anything it became more intense. Julia could tell that its presence meant something terrible to Yuri. He carefully made his way about the apparition, moving as close as he dared, looking for a safe entrance, but each time he seemed to find one the spiral turned and barred his access to it.

'Do be careful, Yuri,' Julia said, catching his arm and holding on to it as he passed her. 'You might be hurt if you touch it.'

'There must be a neutral point,' Yuri muttered to himself and gently eased his arm away from Julia. 'There must be a place where it can be neutralised,' then he fancied he saw just such an opening. Yuri reached his hand out towards it and the children instinctively stepped back. With a bright flash and loud 'pop' Yuri was hurled out of the circle. The apparition disappeared.

He lay so still and cold the younger children ran towards Diana's garden screaming and shouting at the tops of their voices. Julia tried to find Yuri's pulse as she had been taught at school and took off her cardigan to wrap it over his shoulders. Diana was lying on the settee in the living-room after another attack of her voice, when four hysterical young children bounded in through the French windows as though Daphne's hounds were after them. Unable to understand anything they blurted out in disjointed sentences she hastily followed them into the garden and looked out into the meadow where Julia was stooping over Yuri.

'The fairies did it . . . The fairies did it . . .' Vicky kept saying over and over again, and the other three youngsters kept chipping in with equally unhelpful information.

'Something stunned him, Mum,' Julia told her, immediately sensing that it would not be wise to blurt out the whole truth too soon. 'He's terribly cold.'

Diana knelt down to feel his skin. 'Fetch the blanket off the settee, Julia. When he starts coming to we'll get him inside.'

'Is he very bad?' inquired Tom, who had already removed his top hat as though in anticipation of the worst.

'He'll be all right, Tom. I've seen him in a worse state than this.'

'Shall we run and fetch Dr Spalding?' Vicky asked.

Knowing a visit from that gentleman might result in making his condition worse or at the best leaving him with another dose of tranquillisers, Diana told her, 'No, I don't think that will be necessary.'

As soon as the blanket arrived, she wrapped it round him and waited with fingers on his pulse until his eyes slowly began to flicker open.

'Right, children,' Diana announced. 'The emergency is over. I think you can all go home now while Julia and I take him inside.'

Reluctantly, Lin, Kitty, Vicky and Tom took their leave, looking back over their shoulders to see Yuri helped to his feet and guided into the living-room. As soon as he was escorted to the settee, Yuri's rigid body was suddenly overtaken by an attack of shivering which could have been diagnosed as the D.T.s by a less charitable person than Diana. At that moment she wished he would drink something that left a more obvious trace on his breath. Then she could confirm beyond all doubt that his collapse had been due to alcohol rather than being stunned by irritable fairies. Repeatedly wrapping the blanket more securely round him as he kept trying to pull it off, Diana pushed Yuri down on to some cushions and waited until he was capable of uttering words in English. As soon as he showed signs of wanting to make sense, Julia was sent to fetch another pint of milk.

'What on earth have you been drinking, Yuri?' were the first distinct words he heard.

'Drink . . .' he murmured unsurely, 'I drink nothing . . .'

'Well, you wouldn't have passed out like that without some reason. Are you sure you haven't been drinking after taking some of Spalding's tranquillisers?'

'I do not take tranquillisers either. I was right Diana' . . . I was right . . .'

'Right, Yuri? What about?' she asked, unable to relate his murmurings to what he had told her the other day.

'It is terrible . . . This could mean the destruction of the

Earth . . .'

'Oh, Yuri . . . Wake up, you silly man. You only fainted.'

She waved some smelling-salts under his nose and he gasped himself to full consciousness, but far from pacifying him, they seemed to make him worse. 'There can be little time now . . .' Yuri persisted, pushing himself up from the settee. 'We must stop it, we must stop it.'

'Stop what, you dumb-bell? Nothing terrible is going to happen. You dreamt it all.'

'I saw it, though. I reached to touch it . . . It must be stopped.'

Diana was used to Yuri's strange flights of fancy, and because he was not behaving rationally, took his raving to be nothing serious. She would not let him move from the settee until he was much calmer and Julia had returned from the shop.

'What did happen out there, Julia?' she asked her daughter.

Julia took a careful look at Yuri, then at her mother, and was not sure what to say, so she thought the only thing for it was to tell the truth.

'There was something in the fairy ring. It came up through the earth . . .'

'Oh, Julia . . .' Diana sighed in exasperation. 'Can't you see I'm trying to calm Yuri down, not make him worse?'

Steeling herself to look her mother in the eye, Julia continued, 'We were playing in the ring, and Mrs Trotter had just been talking to Yuri . . .' She hesitated as she heard her mother sigh. 'When I was dancing round with Vicky, Tom and the twins, something started to move inside the ring. Yuri came down and reached out to touch it. It was like a four-sided pattern growing from the ground.'

'Oh, Julia . . . Why are you always trying to cover up for Yuri? He's not going to get into any trouble if you tell us what really happened. I don't suppose it had anything to do with Mrs Trotter, did it?' she added as an afterthought when she remembered the inbred expression of her horse.

'Oh, no . . . She had gone some minutes before.'

'All right,' Diana surrendered, 'I won't make you tell me if you don't want to. He's obviously going to live, but we'll have to keep an eye on him until he calms down.'

It took a good few hours before Yuri would calm down and was capable of being taken back to his cottage. Diana made him eat a meal, and, with the promise that she would drop in later that evening to see if he was feeling any better, she returned to her own world of hot flushes and the alien voice. 'Moosevan,' she kept thinking to herself, even when the name was not being pushed into her brain. 'Who or what can Moosevan be?' As she reached the fairy ring where Yuri had collapsed, she inexplicably felt the urge to give it a very wide berth.

5

In a remote corner of an even remoter galaxy a plot to provide an antidote to the bellicose empire-building Mott was being hatched. Reniola and Dax waited apprehensively at the controls of their spacecraft. They were apprehensive that the expansive Mott might have surveillance patrols even in this secluded solar system, and even more concerned that their mysterious accomplices would not keep the rendezvous on the deserted planet. As far as the two Torrans knew, these entities had to come from the next galaxy, and as no other galaxy was visible with the most powerful telescope, it would have been no surprise if they did not make it. But in the safety of their hidden home the Torrans had at last solved the riddle of the Jaulta Code, and the Old Ones were duty bound to answer the message the solution provided. How a transmission from a pretty insignificant satellite could be picked up on the other side of the universe was beyond them, but that had been how the answer to the galaxy's greatest enigma told them to send it. What the message was, remained a mystery to even Reniola and Dax. For fear of it falling into the wrong hands only one terminally ill Torran was allowed to know and transmit it. Then, when they knew the Old Ones had received it, all the deciphering and evidence involved had been sealed in an impenetrable monument to the centuries of effort.

As Reniola and Dax left the comfort of their ship to investigate two flittering forms which passed in front of it, a light shower of carbon dioxide particles floated gently down through the thin air. The tall creatures clothed in atmosphere suits stood waiting patiently on the barren rocky ground as the glimmering shapes came closer and closer. First they spiralled about each other in dainty pirouettes as though looking for some suitable place to rest, then having come to the rim of a small crater they perched on the edge of it and waited.

'Why don't they say something?' Reniola whispered awkwardly to Dax.

'Give them time, give them time. They have probably never known anything like us Torrans before. Even they must be cautious that we aren't laying some sort of trap.'

'But we deciphered the Code. Why should they be suspicious?'

'I think they want us to remove our suits,' Dax pondered carefully.

'If it's all the same to you, I prefer to stay alive,' Reniola insisted. She stood and concentrated for a second. 'Yes, you're right. I can hear them. Now what do we do?'

'As they say I suppose. We've come this far, so it would be daft not to trust them now.'

'Which do you think will happen first? Suffocation or freezing?' Reniola asked, but the sound again seemed to reassure them. 'Oh, all right. I suppose since I chose this stupid little planet I should be the one to find out.'

'I don't see the point in that. Someone will have to get back to the others to tell them that we succeeded. Keep your suit on and watch what happens. I'm due to die because of the mark the Mott put on me anyway.'

'Oh, all right . . .' Reniola agreed reluctantly. 'They must know what they're asking, though.'

Slowly, Dax released the clips holding her helmet to the light suit and she could feel the draught of cold seep through the resulting gap. However, the atmosphere somehow seemed to equate with that inside her suit. With more confidence she pulled the suit apart and stepped out of it. Then she removed her helmet and unfastened her tail to let it sway in an unnatural gentle breeze that ruffled her fine mane. As she stood on long legs before the visitors perched on the rim of the crater she sensed that they were pleased with what they saw. Trying to increase their confidence, Reniola took off her suit and helmet to reveal her more portly proportions. They stood and waited. Occasionally their long muzzles sniffed the atmosphere in curiosity, and their crimson eyes lit up in anticipation and suspense.

The two visitors above them started to rotate within their indistinct transparent bodies very slowly. Soon two shapes could be seen forming, and before Dax and Reniola had time to glance at each other they were staring ahead in disbelief. Accurate in form and every feature, they found themselves gazing at exact replicas of their own bodies.

'You have achieved much,' the taller, more slender shape said. 'Now you must return to your people.'

'But I have the mark on me,' Dax protested. 'It will let the Mott know wherever I am while it's transmitting, and when it stops I will die.'

'Do not worry about the Mott,' said her double. 'We have removed the mark. For the sake of this venture and your own safety you must now cease to exist in name. You will assume new identities. We are now Reniola and Dax.'

'But don't you want to know more about why we had to break the Jaulta Code?' protested Reniola.

'The fact that you did is enough,' the new Dax told her. 'That gives us the ability to trace all members of different species with sensitivities like your own. We shall endeavour to evacuate all who deserve preservation. That is our function. As this galaxy gutters out in many millions of years from now only waste material will die with it.'

'But where do we go to?' the old Dax asked. 'Where did you come from?'

'As I explained, there are millions of years yet to deal with the survival of the Torrans and like-minded species. Our main concern now is for those who will never have your mobility. Do you object to us using your forms?'

'Why should we?' asked the old Reniola. 'We hardly expected to live this long.'

'Life as you know it is not as important as you may believe,' the new Reniola explained. 'But the substance of evolution, however primitive, must always carry on. As stars dwindle and explode to revert to the matter that will form more stars, much of it is not used but drifts aimlessly in space. The same happens to the products of the stars, life itself. Not all life-forms improve in time. There are always some which retrogress in the absence of more advanced kindred. By withdrawing from the galaxy when we did we left the dregs of stagnant evolution. A few like yourselves managed to improve reasonably well despite this and only someone with that evolution could have managed to break the Jaulta Code. With so many stars gone it was inevitable a struggle for what we left would ensue.'

'Can we help you in any way?' asked the old Dax hopefully.

'You have done as much as can be reasonably expected of you,' her double replied. 'All we wish is that you withdraw from the attention of others so we can operate in these guises. It might be that what we have to do will endanger you more than you could have believed possible.'

'Oh, we don't mind that,' the old Reniola chirped, almost relieved that she would have a dash of excitement to live with for the rest of her life. But the old Dax, having just been saved from the inevitable death of the mark, was content enough to follow instructions.

'All right,' she agreed. 'I shall be known as Clyn, and Reniola as Holia. Those names are so common they are protection in themselves.'

'That is good. We are now Dax and Reniola. When we are believed dead, those names will die too.'

'But will you die?' the new Clyn protested.

'No,' Dax assured them. 'We have outlived such clumsy points of evolution as death and birth. Now you must put your suits on and go.'

'But you must tell us what is going to happen,' Holia insisted. 'They'd cut our tails off if we didn't have something to tell them when we got back.'

'You need not concern yourselves from now on,' Dax told

them. 'You have fulfilled your side of the contract.'

'She's trying to say that after centuries of mental sweating over that massive problem, the Torrans should have some idea not only of why you set it, but what you propose to do now it's been solved.'

Dax and Reniola conversed mentally for a short while, before Dax replied, 'We must contain the ambitions of your most aggressive species, and preserve the ones who are being exploited from further suffering. Only then will we decide who is suitable for eventual transference. How we will do this is yet to be decided.'

'We could give you a few starters,' Holia told her enthusiastically.

'Thank you, but we already have access to your memories,' was Dax's sober reply.

'Oh yes . . . of course. I suppose we can retire now then.'

'No. Just be careful,' Reniola advised.

'I think the atmosphere's getting a little thin,' Clyn said as she shivered. 'Cold too.'

'We're being told to go,' Holia said.

Without another word Holia and Clyn pushed their manes and tails back into their suits and helmets and with one last look walked back to their spacecraft.

'Seems strange there wasn't any more it,' commented Holia. She eased the craft out of the thin atmosphere and towards the more agreeable climate of their own world, hidden from the prying eyes of the Mott within the centre of a huge and apparently gaseous planet.

'Can't say I'm complaining about not meeting those over-limbed sabre-toothed Motts,' disagreed Clyn, then smiled. 'My goodness, this is really going to upset them . . . and they won't even know it isn't us.'

'Mind you, it would be enjoyable to see just what they intend to get up to. The idea of all those gallant warriors being beaten up by a couple of pacifists appeals to me.'

'With their powers, they won't need to worry about being violent. Mind that planetoid, can't you, I want to get back alive

48

to enjoy this.'

'Damn junk everywhere,' Holia complained. 'Ever since the Mott blew those planets up this route has been an obstacle course.'

'That was only because they were too pretty for them.'

'Never. It was because they couldn't make any strategic use of them and weren't going to leave them for anyone else to colonise.'

'What a waste with the way things are now. There are too few habitable planets as it is.'

'Haven't you heard the latest?' Holia chuckled as she swerved the craft to avoid another chunk of debris.

'No, what?'

'They are going to shake the planet creatures from their homes with a space-distort net invented by a friend of yours.'

'The planet creatures?' Clyn responded in disbelief. 'That's impossible. I don't know anyone intelligent enough to invent a device which could.'

'Not even that lovable green Kulp?' Holia reminded her.

'I'm glad I changed my name. Now at least I won't have to admit to ever knowing that arrogant poisonous slime squirt.' She shuddered. 'Four tours of the K 49 cluster I did with him, then he decided to turn me over to the Mott when he knew the price was right. Did you know they grew him in a jar under a grey light?'

'No, really?'

'Yes. The Olmuke forgot how to reproduce ages ago. They just keep using the stock of sperm and eggs they collected before females were banned.'

'You must have come as a juddering shock to him.' Holia laughed.

'No . . . I just confounded him a little. At first he thought I was some mechanical variation on an obsolete automaton. Then he discovered that I was living. That's what really upset him. Can't stand to be made a fool of. Hides everything that goes through his evil calculating brain very well though. His planet didn't realise what he'd do when they withheld a grant for him to develop a solar blaster.'

'What did he do?' asked Holia.

'Developed an invisible atmosphere dye instead,' Clyn explained. 'He sprayed it over five major cities, so when their inhabitants went into the sunlight they turned bright pink. And you can guess how much they would love that colour. There was no antidote for it, so a quarter of the planet's population have to spend their days under shelter or turn pink and become social outcasts.'

'Very nasty. But you've got to admit it does have a little style.'

'I've no doubt the infernal contraption he's invented to dislodge the planet creatures will have even more "style". Of all the inoffensive individuals to start on they couldn't have picked a more harmless.'

'It's not as if they can even flee to safety. None of them can exist without their planet.'

'Unless . . .'

'Of course,' Holia smiled. 'I wonder . . .'

The ribbons of vapour parted slightly to let their spacecraft slip through the shell of the seemingly gaseous planet. Down and down into the massive giant they sped to the small terrestrial world at its centre.

'What do you mean? Double the price!' the multi-footed creature with the dental problem spluttered. 'Why didn't you tell me that when you first came in?'

'I'm sorry I made you behave reasonably under false pretences,' Kulp sneered. 'But how do you think I can manage to isolate that collapsar under the original system? If you don't like it, there is a chance I could find another buyer.'

If that did not sweeten the Mott's temper, it at least stopped his abuse in mid flow. That planet was strategically vital to the Mott's conquest of several star clusters, and to lose it to a higher bidder would not endear him to his superiors. But he had to get the price down somehow.

'Why don't we make a compromise,' he said, as his four feet

shuffled his shape of all body and little brain uneasily about the implacable Kulp. 'Can't you drop a few terminals and tighten the net a little?'

'That would mean having one on the planet's surface,' Kulp reminded him, 'and if you want it to be habitable after Moosevan has gone it could be risky.'

The Mott weighed up the risk against what it could save in cost and immediately decided. 'That's what we'll do then, and it'll be on your ugly head if it goes wrong.'

Kulp said nothing. He preferred the thick-skulled creature to go on underestimating him, and the watching Jannu and Tolt were just relieved they had not resorted to anything more violent than words.

'How predictable are things down there?' Jannu asked apprehensively, not ignorant of the potential danger in going to the planet's surface.

'It hasn't moved for the last few years or so,' the Mott replied without any trace of sentiment that could be called scientific. 'Though once it realises what we're up to it might well start thrashing about. I know I'm not going down there.'

'Spoken like a true fearless warrior,' said Kulp.

'You're the one that's paid to be fearless,' snapped the Mott. 'You've got too much invested in your own self-importance to believe anything could happen to you.'

'I know what I'm doing. Unlike anyone else who has tried to tackle this before.'

'I won't say you'd better be right,' added the Mott, 'because I've no doubt you are. But survival doesn't always depend on being right,' he threatened.

'We'll see, we'll see,' Kulp grinned provokingly. 'Malice, to my way of thinking, is a waste of time. Self-preservation is more my philosophy.'

Although Kulp and the Mott commander could be considered as being equally objectionable, their reasoning was species apart. What the Mott could achieve out of pure malice and greed, Kulp could achieve far better out of greed alone without the encumbrance of any other emotion. This green engineer had all the lack of charm that could give orphans a bad name. Kulp did not believe any mortal or immortal Nemesis would descend on him for his sins. He had been the agent behind so many outrages inflicted on unsuspecting and innocent people, and his spacecraft was the fastest his ill-gotten gains could buy. His associates, like Jannu and Tolt, were cowardly to the point of being easy to manipulate and it was a simple matter to predict their actions. At that moment they would be bumbling around in one of the freighter's robot controls talking about everything they would not dare say in front of him.

'What a way to spend this quarter's festival,' complained Jannu as he jarred his unfortunate robots back into life once again.

'Don't worry,' Tolt reassured him. 'After they discover we've teamed up with Kulp they'll never let us back on the planet again anyway.'

'The last quarter, Tritten's moon was blasted out of orbit and a portrait of the supreme commander was made out of its fragments. It could be seen right across the system when the old supernova was above the pole,' reminisced Jannu. 'I doubt if we'll ever see the like of such things again.'

'The glory of the empire we sold to the Mott and the deterioration in the hatchery stock are the only things we'll have to celebrate from now on. That and how hero Kulp managed to blast numerous creatures from their rightful homes and still leave their planets habitable for the glorious Mott.'

'Are you complaining?' asked Jannu, as he fed in yet more of Kulp's modifications to the unprotesting robots.

'I would be if I could see a better way of life, but there are too many Motts and too many Kulps between us and the nearest civilisation for that to arise.'

'You're beginning to sound like a Torran sympathiser. I'd keep those thoughts dark. You know what Kulp thinks of their species.'

'I had heard, but didn't believe anyone could get the better of our infallible partner.'

'Well, someone did,' Jannu told him in a whisper. 'A Torran female called Dax.'

'Go on.' Tolt lowered his voice as well, so intent on learning the scandal he did not notice the panel in the ceiling slide silently back.

'She was a pilot and co-ordination engineer on a freighter touring the K 49 cluster when he was second in command. He always thought she was synthetic until she used the hold to evacuate some refugees from a planet poisoned by the Mott. Kulp wanted to use the space for more freight and was going to open the hold doors and ditch them, but she managed to get hold of some of the dye he used on our planet. She sprayed it through the ventilator of his room, then altered all the freighter's lighting to shine in the same wavelength as a medium-yellow sun like ours.' Jannu stopped briefly as Tolt began to snigger in his distracting way. 'He couldn't do anything about the refugees after that because he daren't leave his quarters. And what's the betting that when he goes down to that planet he won't want any company?'

By this time Tolt was rolling about in delight and Jannu had to stop feeding the robots information for fear of making a mistake.

'What did he do?' Tolt gasped.

'Oh . . . As soon as he was able to put the lights straight without being seen, he trumped up something to frame the Torran with and handed her over to the Mott. They couldn't understand the complexity of the crime he invented, so they put a mark on her and let her go. He got paid for it though.'

'Trust him to land on his feet,' Tolt sniffed, as his six fingers wiped his tears away. 'I don't suppose Kulp would take kindly to us knowing that one.'

'It'd be sudden death if he thought we did. As long as that Torran lives, so does his moment of ignominy.'

'I'll keep it to myself and relish it whenever he lapses into one of his least bearable moods.' Tolt was too overcome to look up and see the panel in the ceiling silently slide back.

6

As promised, Diana slipped out in the evening to check on Yuri. As she left the cottage where Julia and one of her friends were sitting mesmerised in front of the television and walked across the meadow in the midsummer dusk, she glimpsed two shapes standing by Yuri's cottage. One was very distinctive, had two heads, four legs and was black. The other was equally recognisable, but small, agitated and making the motions of a very enraged Eva. As words of the conversation not so much drifted down, but were blasted towards her, Diana could tell by the tenor of the voices that she should approach with extreme stealth if at all. It was only concern for what had happened to Yuri that did not drive her back inside to mind her own business. She knew Daphne Trotter's attitude towards Yuri, and was partially convinced that Eva's was little better. To have the two women descend on him in his present condition might well make him permanently dependent on tranquillisers and gin.

Fortunately they were so involved in their own exchange of opinions they did not hear her creep closer with the concealing help of some wild rose bushes.

'Don't tell me how to run my affairs, lady muck!' Eva was advising the booted figure towering above her on the black horse. 'I own the lease to this land and am selling it to no one, so there's no need to try any more devious little deals with my solicitor.'

'Be careful how you talk to me,' Daphne threatened darkly.

'Oh, but I am, and I'm enjoying every moment of it. If I catch you on this land, whether it's knocking gates off their hinges or frolicking about in the stinging nettles, I'll have you bound over so fast you won't even have time to recognise yourself in the local rag. I would consider it the crowning achievement of my career to see your fat arse kicked about this county by every person your malevolent claws have sunk themselves in.'

'Have you quite finished?' Daphne just managed to chip in, but not for long because Eva had only stopped for breath before she went on.

'No chance, you racist, blue-bottomed turd. I'm not one of your locally intimidated parishioners. You're likely to have one hell of a job if you start poking around in our territory, up or down, so don't try threatening me again.'

'You and your friend Diana should camp out here together. You're obsessive about your little plot of land and I think she's in love with that mental Russian. She never seems to keep away from him. I don't know, perhaps the feeling's mutual. I'm sure that whatever it is we're not likely to be hearing wedding bells. She's always taken care never to marry before.'

'Leave her name out of this, flint features. Just because your husband made a mistake and thought the dowry was worth it doesn't make you any morally superior. If a good thought ever did cross your mind it would probably never get any further than your backside and then it would escape through the hole in your knickers.'

A strangled sound escaped from the larger silhouette, and it could either have been Daphne gurgling in rage or the horse passing wind.

'You are mad, woman!' Daphne's shrill voice suddenly shrieked. 'You have no right to talk to me like this.'

'Do something about it then, you whining fox tormentor, but just be careful someone doesn't come knocking at your stable door for the damage the hunt do to the telescope tracks.'

'You can't prove that.'

'We will when we electrocute one of you bleeders.'

'What do you mean?'

'Next time your little party of obese businessmen and

stuck-up nouveaux riches come trip-trapping over our bridge there'll be a few volts running through the track.'

'You wouldn't dare . . . '

'Oh, not enough to hurt the animals or make it illegal or anything terrible enough for you to use as an excuse to close us down, but just enough to make a horse wonder what made its shoes tingle. And even I know what horses do when their tiny inbred brains can't give ready enough explanations.'

'You scruffy, despicable little female . . .' Daphne started to storm, but rage made the words stick in her throat.

'Now, now, compliments will not change our minds. Some of us have this sense of self-preservation brought about by secondary-school education. Our telescopes are more important than your Sunday excursions to assassinate the dwindling wildlife in this neighbourhood. If your wretched building contractors don't build on some poor little bleeder's nesting area, one of you are liable to come after it with a gun . . . Just like that thug Bert Wheeler. If you two had the same accents I wouldn't be surprised if you wore each other's boots.'

Diana had just started to wonder which one was playing the part of Godzilla and which King Kong when Daphne's horse started to show signs of shell-shock. It flicked its tail and swivelled its ears in a spasm of annoyance before advancing sideways down the meadow with Eva shouting after it and its rider, 'And just remember what I said about trespassing on this land, you jack-booted crow!' The horse beat a hasty retreat to take Daphne out of earshot before she could add any more.

Remaining concealed, Diana pondered why Eva had never mentioned the fact that she had the lease of Yuri's cottage. She was even more mystified when she turned to walk to the door of the cottage which had been left open because of the warm night air. Never having ever spied on anyone before, Diana silently made her way past the partially dismembered gate and peered into the main room. Eva was still too steaming with the exertion of combat and Yuri was too drunk to notice her.

She watched in amazement as Eva prised a gin bottle from the vice-like grip Yuri had on it and poured herself a substantial swig of the stuff in an enamel mug.

'You disgusting, addled little astronomer,' Eva commented in a strange affectionately exasperated way, then hiccuped at having drunk the gin too rapidly. 'Hell . . .' she sighed, 'what on earth possessed you to believe that stupid woman? The one about the apparition in the fairy ring had more sense in it than that . . . are you listening to me?' she demanded at the top of Yuri's head which was slumped on the table. The grey frizzy locks lifted themselves briefly so their owner could say, 'It does not matter . . . nothing matters . . .' Then gravity took over and his head hit the table with a thump.

'Couldn't you think up something more cheerful than the end of the world?' Eva went on. 'If I have to come and spend hours listening to you babbling on I'd occasionally like to hear something with laughs in it.'

Again Yuri endeavoured to sit upright, and when he had partially succeeded, Diana could see the bleary expression on his face which he only usually wore when he was unconscious. 'You are practical,' he murmured. 'Why not laugh at the thought of the world being blown apart?'

'Are you trying to drive me crackers as well? When you're like this you really have to be taken in small doses. If Spalding ever had a case of incurable optimism on his hands he could prescribe you.'

'Still you will not believe me . . .' Yuri smiled cynically. 'I wish I could think myself as crazy as you do. I would not have to believe it then.'

'But it isn't true, Yuri. You're tormenting yourself over nothing. It's all such a pointless waste.'

'To you I owe everything . . . I am nothing but albatross round your neck, but you treat me good. All this I would surrender if you would just this once believe me . . . Check my findings . . .' he pleaded, 'you are one of the few that could.'

'But I thought it was too late by your calculations? Isn't the world going to be shattered by this infernal device the day after tomorrow or something? What benefit would anyone, human or alien, gain by reducing the Earth to rubble, for pity's sake?'

Yuri rolled his head in a sudden surge of drunken stupor as though no longer wanting to hold on to the reality of the conversation and swayed out of his chair to snatch up a handful of exercise books.

'Everything . . . everything . . . Mrs Daphne; little Julia; big Diana; radio telescopes; Dr Eva; me; Sydney Harbour Bridge; Albert Hall; Siberia; all the camels in Egypt; and the pyramids . . .'

'Stop it, Yuri,' Eva said firmly, but he carried on regardless.

'All the whisky in Scotland; Royal family; all the foxes they chase; Ukrainian wheat harvest; Big Wheel in Vienna; all the reindeer in Lapland; the Sahara Desert; English Channel; Chinese take-away shop; all the igloos in Greenland . . .' at this point Eva rose to go to him. '. . . All the pretty dresses in Paris; fountains in Rome –' She slapped his face with enough force to convince him she had meant what she said.

'Eva . . .' Diana protested.

Hardly surprised at her sudden appearance, Eva calmly assured her, 'He'll only get worse if I let him go on.'

Yuri collapsed back into the chair still clutching the exercise books and looking as though he was likely to topple to the floor at any moment.

'But he doesn't get like this very often. He should have the chance to sleep it off.'

'When I arrived he'd been using most of the time to drink it off.'

'But he was all right when I left him. Did you know he collapsed earlier on?'

'No. It doesn't surprise me after what he's been ranting on about, though.'

'Apparitions in fairy rings?' inquired Diana.

'That's the latest. At least it makes a change from accreting planetoids, I suppose. Getting a message from the switchboard to say he wants to see me about apparitions in fairy rings does not exactly work wonders for your prestige when you know it's been passed round to everyone else before you see it.'

'He phoned you about it?'

'Partly my fault, I suppose. It was my idea to have the phone installed.' Eva looked straight at her friend. 'I had to marry him.'

Amazement that her logical friend could have made such a miscalculation showed in Diana's expression, so Eva explained, 'To save him from being deported.'

'What, you?' Diana gasped in disbelief at the thought she was capable of such tender emotions.

'Nobody else would. Three of us agreed to draw straws, but the other two chickened out when they discovered his brain was as soft as his looks. He came over with a group of scientists fifteen years ago. They all decided to ask for political asylum and it was granted, all barring Yuri's. He didn't know anything strategic enough to make him worth the while, you see. The only thing he had to worry about in going back was spending the rest of his life in an asylum. He was a bit eccentric even then. Had some strange ideas in those days as well. You get strange ideas where he comes from and they put you away for it.' Then she shrugged. 'He's always been totally harmless, though. Only wanted his reflector and somewhere to watch the sky. Barring a few minor outbursts he'd always been so well-behaved until recently. Now he's developing into a right headache.'

'Eva . . . there couldn't be anything in what he says could there?'

'No, no,' groaned Eva. 'It's you and your voice next is it?'

'It was just a thought.'

'For pity's sake leave them to Yuri. One day he might find a real use for them. If I spend the night here, will you call in some time tomorrow morning?'

'Of course. He will have calmed down by then, though.'

'I don't know,' Eva sighed. 'This time he really believes it's the end of the world. As if that Trotter woman wasn't enough already.'

'What was she up to then?' asked Diana, not wanting to admit she had heard their reverberating conversation.

'Because her horse dumped her in our stinging nettles she thought she would try some underhand dealings with my

59

solicitor to get the lease on this property. I bought it years ago for Yuri so I could keep an eye on him and he could have a clear view of the sky. My solicitor is straight, though. I thought it was about time that Trotter woman stopped terrorising Yuri, so I told the man to tell her to come here, only she didn't expect to see *me*.'

'Oh?' asked Diana innocently.

'It's unlikely she'll be bothering us again,' Eva added laconically. 'Now all we have to do is exorcise his fairy apparitions.' She thought carefully for a few seconds as a wicked idea crossed her mind. 'You wouldn't like to marry him, would you?'

Never having regarded Yuri as anything but amiably crazy the invitation took Diana unprepared. 'But there wouldn't be any point, would there?' she stammered. 'It's not as if . . .'

'No, you're right there. I've never had any passionate encounters with him over the past fifteen years. He's always been too busy wondering about close encounters, when the stars were going to collide and how the end of the world would come.'

'Then why didn't you divorce him?'

'Because I'm not so passionate myself and the Mrs Trotters of this world would have put him in an asylum long before now if I had stopped supporting him. He can't be left to his own devices for too long. You know what happens if he is.'

'Fancy not saying anything about this to me for all these years, though. How on earth did you manage to look after him without me seeing you?'

'Practised stealth. That and the fact I didn't want anyone to know I was married to him. I've got a career to think about, you know.'

'I didn't believe you thought about anything else.' She laughed. 'Fancy you being married.'

'Shut up, Mog, and help me put him to bed,' Eva said, obviously not as overjoyed at the arrangement as her friend.

'Though come to think of it, it isn't all that surprising after all. You're both right little scruffs.'

'That's as may be. But we're clean. I make sure his clothes are washed and dry before he puts them on, and you wash them again when he's wearing them.'

Unable to deny that, Diana helped to humour and put to bed their mutual problem. When that was done she was about to leave Eva drinking the rest of the gin out of the enamel mug, but retreat was not that easy.

'Put the cover over the reflector as you go out, will you, Mog?' Eva called after her, not realising how anxious she was to escape before she stumbled on something else that would keep her awake all night.

'All right,' sighed Diana, and spent the next twenty minutes looking for the tarpaulin in the garden, unravelling it into submission and hurling it over the telescope with the expertise she used to make beds.

The revelation of Eva's unlikely marriage quite usurped the concern for Yuri's condition from Diana's mind. It was not until she was lying in bed that night that she realised how fragile the balance of anyone's mind could be. In the warm midsummer night air she suddenly felt the surge of another flush which she knew would leave her with a wringing wet nightdress. Unable to ignore it by lapsing into sleep and too tired to get up and wash it away with the half-bottle of sherry she had left over from a cake she had made, Diana tried to fix her gaze on the darkened ceiling. The pretty pastel posies about her were still visible, though withered into shades of grey. The creams, sprays and make-up on the dressing-table created a sinister outline, and the bedclothes became an encumbrance which aggravated her sweating condition. Then came the sudden flashes of kaleidoscope colours before her eyes, followed closely by a buzzing more aggressive than a hive of enraged bees. Then, as though those symptoms were not enough, the inevitable, 'Moosevan . . . Moosevan . . . Why won't you answer?' Suddenly Diana was sitting bolt upright in horror. In the unfamiliarity her bedroom had decided to assume the message was chilling and real.

'I am ready now . . .' it went on inside her mind. 'This is

61

Moosevan . . . There is little time left . . . You must respond . . .'

'Why? . . . Why? . . . Why?' Diana suddenly found herself calling out in exasperation, then clamping her hand over her mouth for fear of waking Julia, but as she did so she realised that her words were not coming from her throat. 'What do you want?' her mind was calling back to the intruder. 'Who are you?'

It seemed as though that took her caller by surprise, because she could only sense the faint crackle of its presence before the words eventually came back.

'My name is Moosevan,' it said, as though she should have known that already. 'Who are you?'

'I am Diana,' she replied with a part of her brain she never realised she had before. 'What do you want?'

'I must have my world very soon, or it will be too late,' was the strange answer.

'But I haven't got your world.'

'Something is stopping it from coming together.'

'What could that be?'

'You must tell me. I will perish without it.'

'If there is something stopping it from coming together there must be a reason. But I don't know it . . .' Diana began to think hard, despite the absurdity of the conversation. 'Or do I . . .'

'Think, Diana,' Moosevan purred persuasively.

'Yuri told me . . . but I didn't understand.'

'Sleep. I will take it from your mind where you cannot reach.'

'I can't. I have trouble sleeping.'

'You are hot, Diana . . . This is not right.'

Unable to give the reply her tongue might have used, Diana's mind replied, 'I am not well.'

'But why are you a living entity?' The voice sounded confused. 'And this language is alien to me.'

'Am I still living?' Diana asked.

There was a long ponderous pause again before the voice came back, 'May I reach into your mind?'

'Yes,' replied Diana, 'I want to sleep.' No sooner had she thought those words than she could feel her eyelids closing as she sank from her rigid posture on to the feather pillow.

7

With a clunk and a squeaking, screeching sound that set the Mott's tusks on edge, Kulp released the hundred and tenth beacon. As the Mott commander had shown little trust in Kulp by demanding to watch the vital exercise, Kulp was getting his own back by bringing the squeaking down to such a fine pitch that the Mott sensed he would soon become a dentist's nightmare.

'Do you have to do that?' he snapped in exasperation after the one hundred and twentieth beacon had been released. 'I'm pretty sure your efficiency could have eliminated that noise long before now.'

'Time to adjust such a minor thing would be money,' Kulp reminded him, 'and I'm sure a little thing like that is not going to distress a Mott commander who has been in the thick of the most bloody confrontations seen on this side of the galaxy.'

There was no reply to that, so the Mott just squinted his eye in pique and backed away from the infernal equipment emitting the tooth-shattering sound. He also began to feel nauseous because of the rich atmosphere Jannu, Kulp and Tolt had saturated their ship with. Although all life-forms had been compelled to adapt to one standard atmosphere, the many variations on it could cause great discomfort to those unused to them. The Mott stamped each of his four feet in turn as he realised it would be some while before he was released from their doleful company. If he had the choice he would have preferred chasing the backward tribes on some dingy little planet on the edge of nowhere with a flash blaster. Unfortunately for him those balmy days of carefree pleasures were over. Most of the evolving tribes had to stop evolving to join sides with the Mott so they could have flash blasters of their own.

The two hundred and twenty-fifth beacon juddered into its prearranged piece of space from the faulty evacuation shute below them, and Kulp announced with a degree of disappointment in his voice, 'That's all for that quarter. Now we'll have to go down to the planet to install the next terminal.'

'Need any help?' Jannu asked innocently, and nearly fell through the floor when Kulp replied, 'Yes. You and Tolt as well. I don't see why I should do all the work,' then marched out of the control room. Jannu flashed Tolt a quick shrug of the shoulders and Tolt looked just as mystified in return. Could it be that there was a cure for the pink dye after all, or that the story about Kulp's dealing with the Torran Dax had been exaggerated? They had their reply as the intercom snapped on from the dispatch bays and Kulp informed them, 'She's liable to be unstable. Put some suits on.'

'Damn . . .' hissed Jannu, much to the bewilderment of the Mott, and he reluctantly followed Kulp's orders.

As it was in a gravitational field, a robot was not thought necessary to hold the beacon still, but blasting a hole for it to sit in was more difficult than they had accounted for. The planet was sensitive to even such a pinprick and immediately filled in the gaps with as much speed as they could be made. Eventually, Kulp decided to line the next hole with a force field, and this seemed to do the trick. Sliding the beacon down a beam from the freighter's evacuation shute was by comparison a simple matter, and soon there was not much to do but arm it to transmit its devastating signal.

'You sure it's not going to be too much for the planet's crust?' Jannu asked cautiously.

'Of course not,' snapped Kulp. 'Don't you think I know what I'm doing?'

'Of course I do. It's just that we'd like to know once in a

while. How can you be so sure this space-distort net won't kill the atmosphere and everything growing here?'

'I want the Mott to think that's the danger, you idiot. What do you think they would do if they thought the system was foolproof? What would our lives be worth if they thought they could operate it without us?'

'You really think the Mott would double-cross us then?' Tolt asked with an innocence that did not escape Kulp's scheming attention.

'Wouldn't we double-cross them if we had the chance?'

'But that's different,' protested Tolt. 'We're prettier than they are.'

Quite convinced his partner's brain was becoming too soggy to fit the skull the genetic engineers had designed, Kulp wondered whether the effort he had made a short while before to deal with his companions had been worth the trouble.

He had lowered himself to repeat the use of one of his inventions, adapted and increased its strength tenfold, then programmed a minute robot with all the stealth of a common thief to install it. Now it seemed as though his two victims were too dense to appreciate the beauty of the ignominy soon to be unleashed on them. Oh, how Kulp longed for an adversary worthy of his superior mettle. Taking care not to let them wander out of the view he had from his polarised visor, Kulp moved off to check the bearing the signal would follow.

A tinkling shower of gravel and crystals cascaded down the cliff-face and on to the broad leaves of the vigorously growing trees below. The ground heaved and through the ancient trunks a whisper permeated the air.

'Who are these creatures?' it asked. 'They are not the ones I touched . . .'

On the other side of the planet, the tide of one of the small seas suddenly flowed up its shore to flood a field of tall lilies. The one who had words to give her was kind, but the other, who could only feel, enticed her out of her usual tranquillity. So she searched. She parted the forests with an invisible comb and turned over shifting sands, but was still unable to find the object of her fascination. Although she sensed the danger of the three companions with their pricking, irritating machine, her mighty being had its interest absorbed elsewhere.

Ice floes were shaken free from the poles and glaciers pushed leisurely on their ways over ground where ice had never been before. The three intruders sensed the restless changes but still carried on with their task as if unaware of the planet's potential strength.

But Moosevan did not kill. She did not know how. Nor should the need ever arise, but something was very wrong. She had called time and time again, but could receive no sensible answer. The part that should have been the core of her new body was silent and still. Though she knew it was still functioning it would not answer her command. When she reached out with her thoughts through the gate this strange intriguing creature had extended its hand to touch them. She had never known any other sensation fill her with such curiosity. From time remembered, other living things had landed on her temperate plains and come and gone in their flights across the galaxy. Some Moosevan had found amusing and friendly. She had made their temporary homes shimmer with exotic mists. Others were brutal and unreasoning, so she had shifted the ground in undulating ripples to make their stays as unpleasant as possible. Energy life-forms had floated like phantoms through her forests and jungles of twisted vegetation and whispered the secrets of the universe to her, but she had never encountered anything like this one brief touch before.

Since the Old Ones had left, the new species had feared the might of a world that could overwhelm them. Having to respect the very ground they trod on, was too much for the sense of their own self-importance. Moosevan could have accidentally shuddered and split the ground beneath them, but she would never have done such a thing on purpose and she wondered why these three companions were the only ones to come after such a length of time. It was strange that her second contact from the gate should be the total opposite of what these creatures were. Even though the message taken from her mind meant the end of her existence. She had a sympathetic heart, and that was something the planet had long missed.

Moosevan was ageing. She had lived half as long as the now dwindling galaxy, and could not reasonably expect to go on forever. The Old Ones had given her the means to escape, but the cost of using it would be too high. So all she could do was wait. Wait and hope she would again be able to touch that strange entity before passing from her world into infinity. She sighed once more, and a precariously balanced boulder said to the rock outcrop it sat on, 'What is she so restless about?'

'It must be something to do with the beacon those three have just installed,' answered the rock.

'Can't we dissolve it?'

'Wouldn't be any point. They must operate the space-distort net, or we'll have to go through all this again somewhere else.'

'I've got a feeling things are going to get more complicated,' said the boulder, swaying thoughtfully.

'Don't do that. It's unbelievably uncomfortable.'

'Why do we have to sit here like this anyway? It was far more agreeable as we were.'

'Because we have to find out what's going on without them suspecting,' replied the rock irritably. 'If we used those other shapes they would probably forget what they were doing to try and kill us.'

'It's enough to make you realise how fortunate we are not to be mortal, but I would prefer the fur coat again. The mental capacity of this material is somewhat restricting.'

'Forget the fur coat. I just told you one of those creatures would try to assassinate it on sight. Why don't you use the Torran's memory bank?'

'I don't feel like running through it now. I'd much rather roll down that cliff-face and see what their reaction would be.'

'Don't forget I'm underneath here,' the rock reminded it. 'You'll have to learn to be a little more patient. None of us has had to do anything like this for aeons, so it's bound to be a little frustrating.'

'Oh, just a little pitch and tumble won't bring everything to a halt. Tuck yourself in. Here I go,' and away went the boulder with a reverberating crash.

'Where the hell did that come from?' yelped Tolt as he leapt out of the path of an unusually large animated rock that seemed to be chasing his heels.

'The lump probably threw it at us,' Kulp commented drily from a safe distance.

'You can hardly blame her,' said Jannu. 'If someone was trying to distort me from my cosy little shell I'd probably get a bit touchy as well.'

'Will you two stop being so damned reasonable,' snapped Kulp. 'It's beginning to make me nervous.' He opened the casing of the beacon to reach inside it with a torch. 'I'm not going to arm this terminal until the others are in sequence. It'd be too risky with all this turbulence.'

'The atmosphere seems reasonably stable, though,' commented Tolt innocently, not realising Kulp was perfectly aware of what he was driving at.

'Seems very balmy,' added Jannu.

'You two can go for a stroll if you like, but there might not be a shuttle waiting, or a spacecraft to take you off, when I start triggering the net.'

'In that case I don't think I'll bother,' Tolt decided, principally influenced by the knowledge that as the idea of ditching them had crossed Kulp's mind he would undoubtedly take the first opportunity to do it.

With the beacon aligned, and only waiting to be armed in readiness to twist the planet through every distortion that matched its inventor moral sense, Tolt and Jannu followed him back to the shuttle. They were nursing a fair degree of disappointment that they had not thought of some way to make him remove his helmet.

The Mott commander was doing a brisk trot around his observation chamber when the three of them entered to report their progress.

'Why are you taking so much time?' he demanded with a Mott sense of agitation well into third gear. 'I've got to make a report soon.'

'Report away,' Kulp informed him leisurely. 'I'll do things in my own good time and not be rushed by any little ringlet-covered egotist with a personality problem,' and strode out of the chamber without apparently realising the danger in accurately describing a Mott to his face.

Jannu and Tolt remained, not sure whether it was better to keep company with Kulp while he was in that sort of mood, or wait and see what the reaction of the Mott would be. The Mott valued their ringlets above all else, or perhaps almost all else, as they were an indicator of a male's virility and valour next to the first best appendage. Such a comment coming from a hairless, green, toad thing without either, made the Mott growl and stamp with rage until the other two thought he was going to gallop up the wall and across the ceiling. Only taking the precaution of not being in his path when he decided to do it, Jannu and Tolt waited patiently until the Mott had returned to a more rational state.

'He's always been like that,' commented Tolt. 'Don't pay any attention.'

'Somebody gave his jar a vigorous shake when he was still an embryo and it must have affected him,' Jannu added.

'I don't like that creature . . .' gurgled the Mott.

This hardly surprised the other two, because, like the Olmuke, the Mott had never been known to like anyone in recorded history.

'He can be a little trying,' advised Jannu. 'But as long as you keep your eye on him he's not liable to get up to much.'

The Mott was silent for a moment. He waited, sensing that there was something pertinent in Jannu's angling comment.

'What do you mean? What would he get up to if he wasn't being watched?'

'Oh . . .' Tolt pretended to reassure, 'don't worry about it. We're honest enough, and are not likely to go along with him.'

'After all,' Jannu laughed, 'who with any sense of self-preservation would want to cross the Mott?'

'Kulp would,' concluded the Mott with accuracy unusual for

his dull reasoning. 'And how do I know I can trust either of you two?'

'Look . . .' Tolt started carefully, 'if Kulp double-crossed you, then it stands to reason he would be double-crossing us as well.'

'For instance?'

'For instance,' said Jannu, 'just assuming this space-distort net isn't successful: he's got the down-payment on the scheme. You can easily check to see if anything was paid to us.'

'Not an atom, I assure you,' Tolt agreed. 'He has the fastest ship. We've only freighter-class craft and would never be able to outrun the Mott fleet.'

Despite the Mott's natural suspicion, he wanted to believe them, but in so doing he would have to trust members of a different species, and that was as impossible as trusting a Mott female. He clip-clopped about the chamber for a short while, weighing up Kulp's total disregard for a member of the most superior species in the galaxy, with what his seniors would say if they discovered they could not operate the net without its inventor. Tolt had anticipated that difficulty, though.

'*We* know how to operate the net. He's ironed out most of the awkward problems so we won't find it that difficult. All we want him to do now is arm the terminal on the planet, then we won't need him any more.'

'What about Mott engineers?' the commander inquired.

'Well . . .' mused Jannu carefully, 'they did have trouble operating the one they designed themselves . . .'

'We could not guarantee to simplify it to that extent,' added Tolt. 'After all, we weren't the inventors, remember. It would be asking a lot of us.'

'So what do you think Kulp will do?' asked the Mott.

'Do?' laughed Jannu. 'He may decide to keep to the bargain exactly as made.'

'Then again he might not,' said Tolt, 'but we could never do anything unless he showed himself to be totally untrustworthy.'

That was what the Mott commander was hoping. Nothing would please him more than to have the distort-net system *and* the head of the creature that invented it.

'What would you do if he did not prove trustworthy?' he demanded.

Jannu and Tolt looked at each other and shrugged.

'What else could we do but keep to our side of the bargain?' Tolt grinned.

'As long as we get his percentage, of course,' added Jannu quickly.

'What? All of it?'

'What else?' said Jannu firmly, and the Mott could see he was not going to budge on that point.

'Something tells me we might be doing business without a certain fourth party very shortly,' sneered the Mott, his mouth moistening at the prospect of knowing Kulp was fatally wounded if not dead. 'Isn't it strange how allies find each other?'

No longer aggravated by the blasting and probing of the three intruders, Moosevan soon lost interest in them. Had she not been so concerned about finding the object of her fascination, she might have given more of her colossal thought to the problem of what those creatures were about to do. Even if she had, though, there was nothing she could do to stop it, so once again she reached out through the gate. This time her touch was gentle, and did not try to frantically grasp at the mechanism that she knew to be there. Carefully, she wafted strange sensations that were part of herself into the pathway the Old Ones had made for her into another part of the universe.

8

'Of course,' said John, as he scratched his chin which was somewhere concealed beneath the forest growing from it, 'we could always trap the foxes ourselves and release them somewhere else?'

'No good,' argued Fran. 'The chances are they would make their way back here, or be killed by some other hunt or gamekeeper. The real problem as I see it is that hunting must be banned once and for all.'

'Fine chance while the ones in power are the ones who go in for that sort of carnage.'

'But reasonable argument is the only way this problem can be tackled. If we resort to violence then we become the same as them.'

'I still think shoving a few volts through the telescope tracks is a good idea,' John grinned to himself beneath the privacy of his undergrowth. 'Never thought I would ever have anything in common with scientists.'

'They are just as pernicious as the mistakes they make,' Fran cautioned him. 'They are the lackies of the very people that should be removed from power.'

'I wouldn't have thought that small grey-haired woman would go much on hearing you talk like that. From what I heard, she put a flea in the ear of one of the establishment the other night.'

'Apparently most of the village heard her putting more than a flea in the woman's ear,' Fran commented with a degree of distaste only an incurable pacifist could display. 'They were only arguing over property.'

'I think it was something to do with her trying to run all the foreigners out of the village as well. Everyone I've spoken to says Mrs Trotter and her family always have been anti-Semitic, anti-socialist and racist. I don't think they like those telescopes spoiling the local view either. They tried to block the project when the observatory first came. They preferred the museum which reminded them of the old days when the serfs were starving and they occasionally let them have a bushel of their own wheat to survive on.'

At any other time this would have led to a deadly serious philosophical discussion that would have lasted until they reached the museum and probably after, but Fran suddenly stopped and stared across the meadow at the back of Diana's cottage. In the rays of the early morning sunlight something was glimmering and dancing like delicate curtains of dust.

'What on earth is that?' Fran asked. John peered towards where his friend's finger pointed, and commented off-handedly, 'Just a light effect. Could be marsh gas.'

'It doesn't look like that to me.'

'Look . . .' John said earnestly, 'didn't we swear off that stuff?'

'But I haven't touched it. You've been with me all the while so how could I? There seems to be something down there, I tell you. It's moving about like a slowly revolving top, full of shapes and things.'

John took a longer, harder look just to satisfy his companion, but either because he thought Fran was hallucinating or because there was too much hair obscuring his view he insisted, 'It's just a light effect. You're getting like that crazy Russian.'

This immediately took Fran's attention away from the meadow and raised more political sentiments.

'Does he have to be crazy because he's a Russian?' Fran complained.

'The way they have to live must be enough to drive them crazy,' John added against his better judgement.

'How do you know he isn't crazy because he spent half his life in a labour camp?' came the instant response, it somehow not occurring to Fran that the Russian might not be crazy but just maligned by enough people to make it seem fact. 'They said that student was crazy because he insisted he'd seen the Loch Ness monster. And look what happened there . . .'

'So it rained frogs on him while he was walking across the campus. What's that got to do with the Loch Ness monster?'

'It proves that just because somebody claims something apparently impossible, it doesn't mean they are lying,' Fran insisted.

'But we all saw the frogs. We never saw the Loch Ness monster. Anyway, if whatever this Russian fellow keeps going on about is right, it must mean he's sane.'

'Didn't I say that?'

'No,' and the argument went on as they passed by the meadow and into the grounds of the museum.

Still in carpet slippers and dressing-gown at a time she would usually be hard at work in the museum filing something or checking the older wood for rot and beetle, Diana slopped some milk on to a pile of cornflakes and automatically shovelled them down. She dropped the bowl into the sink and scratched her disorganised head through a mop of unbrushed hair as she tried to remember what had hit her in the early hours of that morning. Just as some semblance of order returned to her thoughts, the front doorbell rang. Only stopping off at the mantelpiece to pick up her hairbrush and use it to push the hair out of her face, she swung the door open to see the small figure of the twins' mother.

'Why hello, Cherry.' She smiled, 'Are you about early or did I get up late?' and ushered her through to the living-room.

'I think you are a little late, it's nearly ten past nine.'

'That's late for you maybe. I've got the day off, though. Have a cup of tea.'

'Thank you,' Cherry said, practised in the art of suffering the way the English brewed tea. 'I hope I haven't disturbed you from anything?'

'Only wondering where the rest of me is. Now's the time I

wish I never gave up smoking,' and Diana handed her friend a cup of lukewarm tea.

'You had a rough night?' Cherry inquired carefully, not insensitive to the trauma some women went through when they were much older than herself.

'I'm still not sure when it started or when it ended. I suddenly woke up this morning not only wondering where I was, but who I was as well.'

'Has Dr Spalding . . .?' but the frantic waving of Diana's hand told her she was on dangerous ground. 'Perhaps it was the heat? It was very warm last night.'

'Perhaps . . .' mused Diana, suspecting there was a more sinister explanation for it.

'Is Julia up yet?' asked Cherry, bravely taking a sip at the brown fluid.

'Not her. She plays hard and sleeps hard.'

'Good. I think there is something I should tell you about what happened yesterday.'

'Oh goodness, yes,' remembered Diana. 'It didn't upset the twins did it?'

'Oh no. It was because they were so excited about what happened that it made us wonder.'

'Wonder? I know Yuri doesn't usually make a habit of folding up dead drunk in the middle of the day, but . . .?'

'No, not that. It was what happened inside the ring.'

Diana looked at her in amazement. 'But that was only some story they used to cover up for Yuri. You know what children are.'

'Our children are no less mischievous than anyone else's,' said Cherry, having to admit that the tea had defeated her as she replaced the cup on the tray. 'But as they are twins we have a way of knowing if they are lying or not.'

'Go on,' said Diana with a peculiar feeling of apprehension tingling on her scalp.

'Whenever we think they invent stories, we question them separately. If the story differs in the slightest detail we know they are lying. If they both stick to the same story then we know they are telling the truth.'

Diana looked at her in disbelief and wonderment for a moment before replying, 'You mean to tell me you think that the story about the fairies in the ring is true?'

'We believe they saw what they described to us,' Cherry told her carefully. 'We do not know what it means, of course.'

'If it is true – Julia was telling the truth as well. What did they tell you?'

'They said that they were dancing around inside the ring when the grass started to move. Julia pulled them away from it and they watched as this spiral box full of shapes rose from the ground like solid smoke. Yuri came down and told them to keep away from it, then said something about switching it off. He put his hand inside the ring and the shape knocked him over and disappeared with a flash of light.'

'That sounds like Julia's story. What the hell could it have been?'

'Perhaps there is a generator fault somewhere and it is affecting the electric cables?' suggested Cherry.

Diana shook her head. 'No. I remember the time when that meadow was ploughed regularly. All our water, gas and electricity comes from the street.'

'There must be some explanation for it. That scientist friend of yours could easily explain it.'

Diana flinched inside as she remembered the way she and Eva had poured scorn on Yuri's problem the night before.

'Perhaps Yuri could. I promised to call in and see him later,' she said uneasily.

'He is all right?' Cherry asked.

'Well, he probably slept well last night.'

In fact, Yuri had slept so well the night before that he was up bright and early, and as soon as Eva and the two students had departed to their respective jobs he was down by the fairy ring looking into the mysterious depths of the pattern inside it. Knowing that these shapes marked the entrance to a very long tunnel, perhaps to infinity, Yuri was entranced by the dancing

77

spheres and diamonds. The odd one would now and then break away from its spiral container and flutter towards him like a smoky butterfly, gently touch his face or hand then evaporate with a faint pop. Knowing the clout these inoffensive patterns could deliver, Yuri was not as eager to accept their invitation as he had been before. He did edge closer though, and whatever controlled those plucking parcels of mist seemed to sense both his apprehension and his fascination. Then, feeling the penetration of so many painless bullets he found himself sitting in the centre of a still airless pool. As though he had no need for breath, something had encompassed him like the hand of a colossal giant. It did not grip or close over him though. Yuri could still see the fairy ring and the meadow about it, though they were no longer part of the world he knew. He could feel his body relax as though it had been lowered on to a mattress of down. Without needing to think, somebody else's thoughts slipped into his mind. They did not speak to him, but he could sense an intensity of feeling never known to him before. It was not human, but it was longing. It did not betray its nature, but permeated his body and filled his head with unearthly perfume. Yuri was terrified and elated at the same time. He tried to pull away, but the ring seemed to behave like a magnet and the caress became stronger. His lack of understanding of what it meant soon overcame him and he began to panic. At that the ring slowly began to slacken its grip until he found himself once again sitting in the meadow.

As soon as Cherry had gone, Diana slumped into an armchair and carried out the long overdue reorganisation of her thoughts. She remembered being called by the voice again, and she remembered going to sleep suddenly. But what did she dream about? She knew that to be the vital thing. Flickers of awareness filtered from her subconscious to tell her that something of momentous importance had taken place. She remembered she should have delivered a message of some sort, but what it was totally escaped her as though her conscious thoughts would not let her even guess at it. Then she remembered Yuri, who must have mastered the ultimate in bizarre thoughts. Diana quickly washed and threw on the nearest dress to hand.

Swinging open the back gate she discovered the object of her errand was closer than she might have guessed. Yuri was kneeling beside the fairy ring wearing a strangely blissful expression which expressed nothing of what had happened the day before. He smiled and Diana grasped his outstretched hand to pull him to his feet like a misbehaving child.

'What on earth are you doing out here now?' she asked with a good deal more respect for the ring than she had given it before. 'Are you feeling any better?'

'I feel . . . strange.'

'What happened?' she demanded. Yuri looked at her as though it was unusual for her to take his condition so seriously.

'I do not know. Something came from the ring and touched me.' Expecting Diana to smile patronisingly, his smile faded from his face when she did not. 'I cannot explain it. I have strange head this morning. I think it was gin and Eva last night.'

'Perhaps. Why not come back to your cottage and have some breakfast?'

'Eva makes me eat breakfast. I prefer to stop here.'

'But I want to ask you something, and we can't talk about it out here.'

'But why not?' resisted Yuri, still suffering from the saturating sensuality of the ring. Suddenly he remembered something. 'What day is it?'

'Tuesday.'

'No, I meant what date is it?'

Diana thought for a second as she had not written any cheques or looked at a newspaper for several days.

'Something like the 21st . . . I only know it's the summer solstice either today or tomorrow.'

Yuri's expression of tranquillity changed so rapidly Diana thought she was going to have to catch him before he fell.

'What on earth's the matter? You look as though a tank hit you.'

'Tell me I'm crazy,' Yuri suddenly pleaded, but for once Diana would not oblige him.

'Perhaps you aren't, Yuri. I don't know. But there is something I must try to remember, and you are the only one who can help me do it.'

Yuri looked at her in confusion as though she were some benevolent stranger. 'What should I tell you?' he asked in bewilderment.

'I want you to explain what you discovered from looking at the asteroids.'

'You do not believe me anyway.'

'I don't know, Yuri, but I would like you to do it all the same.'

'All right,' Yuri agreed, suspecting that she might be trying to humour him in some extraordinary way, and as a peal of bells rang out across the fields from the local parish church he led her back up to his cottage.

To conceal his real confusion, Yuri looked as serious as he could. He picked up several exercise books from the floor where he had thrown them the night before and arranged them on the table. For thirty minutes he read out his observations as he thought them relevant to his conclusion as though Diana might have understood them. When the bells suddenly stopped pealing however, he seemed to realise that she was perhaps not humouring him after all. The sudden cessation of the noise seemed to make him aware of a frighteningly empty part of space. Then he could visualise a twisting stream of debris being attracted to form a ring about a small dead planet where the earth's orbit had once been.

'Go on,' Diana gently urged him for fear of his wandering thoughts taking over and making him as unreasonable and incoherent as he had been the night before. 'Tell me what you have found out.'

Yuri sighed. 'I tell you both . . . I tell you . . . I tell you . . .'

'Again Yuri, tell me again,' Diana insisted, and Yuri at last gave in to put into words the fear he had been nursing whether sober or drunk.

'I find planetoids making alignments . . . patterns . . . at certain times of year. Long ago I put this down to coincidence. They were so brief no one else notice it. I make note of these for long while, but planetoids are so difficult to find I have no one to check with. To find one of them you must already know where to look, and to find several on the same night is very difficult. It occurred to me to make out mathematical plots for their future alignments and for many years nothing seemed to happen. Then I discover one big major pattern spread across the sky. It is like pointer and will next be aligned at summer solstice. In line of this there should be another planetoid, but there is not . . .' Yuri stopped.

'So there is nothing there?' Diana prompted.

'There is something there.'

'But what?'

'The Earth.' Yuri said it so simply that the full relevance of it did not immediately seem that terrible. Then Diana remembered Yuri telling her about the way he thought the planetoids would accrete and form another planet. He confirmed her apprehension by explaining, 'According to my calculations there is a large mass missing from the jigsaw pattern.'

'Not the Earth?'

'No . . . not the Earth . . . but something which it accreted around many many millions of years ago when the solar system was forming.'

'But surely everything in the solar system came from matter formed at the same time?'

'There may have been something here in this part of space circling the new sun already. I do not know why it should have been here, but from its point of view, we are the intruders. We are the ones who enclosed part of its body inside our own planet.'

'And you are saying that now that this collection of rock is correctly aligned . . . all it wants to do is follow its original function and come together to form another planet?'

'I get transmitter and equipment from Eva and make signal to probe for its control point. I eventually find right frequency and machine inside body sends its signal out to planetoids and space from meadow down there. I believe the mass is so large that seismologists do not register it as being anything but part of Earth.'

'So you attracted the machine to materialise an image here?' Diana said, amazed that Yuri should have had the ability to achieve anything of this kind.

'It was not difficult to isolate its signal,' Yuri assured her. 'You believe and know where to look, it is quite easy. I'm sure this mechanism has the power to throw the pieces of the jigsaw together within minutes like a giant spring. The momentum of such a happening would rapidly create heat to rend the components into their homogeneous layers and rotation to give it form and gravity. We would disintegrate and the debris not used building the new planet would become flattened stranded discs to decorate it and our moon. There would probably be nothing large enough left to form satellites, but the moon would more than likely gain its liberation and pursue an orbit of its own to become a planet. Two new planets for one old one . . . If I am right I should name them . . .' but Diana knew what names he was about to give them and her warning look made him bite his tongue. 'Of course, there would be little point as we would not be around, not in whole pieces anyway. Some think the planetoids came into being because a planet exploded, but no one but me has yet worked out how a planet could explode. They do not think it possible . . .' He looked sympathetically at her mystified expression. 'Does this help you remember what you wanted?'

The light of realisation had gone on in Diana's mind, but she dared not let Yuri know. What she had been thinking were the throes of age's natural function were in part something a good deal more sinister. She saw Yuri looking quizzically at her and she braced herself to smile without giving the game away. 'I suppose, then, I'd better wait before booking up for next year's holiday if I can't be sure what planet I'll be living on.'

'There . . . you still mock me . . .'

'No, Yuri . . .' she protested thinly. 'But I want you to

promise me something.'

'What is it?'

'Will you do it?'

'What is it?' he insisted with a surprising degree of discernment for one who was supposed to be insane.

'Please stay inside for the rest of the day. You look very tired. You should get some rest.'

'Huh . . . You sound like Dr Eva.'

'Why don't you take a couple of tranquillisers and try to sleep,' she advised, but he grunted again, 'Now you sound like Dr Spalding.'

'Everything will be all right,' Diana assured him, wearing her intensely honest expression, though something in the back of her mind refused to tell her whether Moosevan had understood after all. 'I'll have to be out for the rest of the day and I'm going to send Julia to her cousin's until I return, so if you decide to flake out again there isn't likely to be anyone around to pick you up.'

'Does it matter?' smiled Yuri, quite convinced of his findings and what was inevitably going to happen.

'Please, Yuri,' Diana pleaded with a desperation that even he noticed.

'If you feel that strong, I do it. I would sooner die drunk in here, than sober out there.'

'It'll be all right,' she assured him, but he did not understand she knew even more than he did, and would not have believed it if she had told him.

Unable to think of some way to dope Yuri without his knowing, Diana was compelled to return to her cottage and tip her sleeping daughter out of bed. With strict instructions to stay out of the meadow and the key to the front door she packed her off to her cousin's. Making herself as tidy as possible and reviewing the contents of her handbag, Diana put the will she had made and had witnessed months ago into an envelope. She wrote the address of her solicitor on it, affixed a first-class stamp, put it in her handbag, and left to post it.

9

For some while Yuri genuinely tried to obey Diana's orders, but if he was able to control his restlessness about the impending end of the world, the encounter with the strange intellect in the meadow below filled his head with very odd desires. One moment he wished for nothing more than to be able to dismiss them from his tumbling thoughts, and in the next the only thing he wanted to do was rush down to the fairy ring and call them into life again. Until that morning he had not known the true meaning of confusion.

In frustration, Yuri dashed about his cluttered living-room, snatching up exercise books, textbooks and anything that could be stacked into a pile with them. These he crammed into the already overflowing bookcase whether they belonged there or not. Cushions were pounded back into shape. Vases, plates and ornaments were thrown into the sink and scrubbed clean of any ancient patterns that had managed to cling to them. The table was rapidly waxed and polished, legs, struts and all, armchairs and sofa pounded until every speck of dust from years past had given up its hold. This was a lot of dust, and the resulting attack of sneezing drove Yuri into the garden where he made his way to the coal-bunker.

Rummaging about in the part where he kept the unused garden tools Eva had bought him, he eventually pulled out a scythe. It was practically free from rust and as sharp as the day it was purchased. He was reluctant to assault the stinging nettles at the bottom of the garden as they had done him such a favour in molesting the pompous Daphne Trotter. Yuri nevertheless reasoned that his state of desperation was greater than his gratitude and began to set about them with the ferocity of a true madman. With arms stung more than Daphne's extremities, Yuri ploughed on regardless until he was actually able to see the fence that bordered the property.

Exhausted, he slumped down in the middle of the felled weeds and pulled off his shirt to reveal a shabby T-shirt and a haphazardly tied neck-scarf which was too worn to serve any useful purpose. He rubbed his arms ruefully as he looked about him for something else to attack. Still the urge to go back to the ring gnawed at him. He pulled his fob-watch out of his trouser pocket and discovered that he had managed to kill only forty minutes. It was not even midday. Perhaps if he phoned Eva . . .? She would be mad and driven one step nearer to having him certified and not be the best company to spend one's last day on earth with. Diana had gone and deserted him the very day he needed to be convinced of his insanity the most.

Perhaps the world was only coming to an end in his head and the strange experience in the ring a symptom of that encroaching madness? That must be it. He was a scientist and should use what sense he had managed to cling to in rationalising his hysterical thoughts. But he had collected his data over the years in a thoroughly scientific, though increasingly inebriated, way and his rational sense told him from it that it was inevitable the Earth would explode at any moment. Whether he dropped dead then and there or lived for another hundred years did not bother Yuri. It was the people he knew that he grieved for. Diana, little Julia and her friends . . . and even Eva. How could the thing that had held him so gently in its phantom hand be the very thing which was going to destroy them?

An idea filtered into his jumbled brain. What if he could contact it and make himself understood? He shuddered. There were many ways to be killed, and he knew several of them from uncomfortably close experience. The idea of being crushed in the palm of an unknown being with perfumed thoughts permeating his every cell again filled him with the fearful fascination that had been trying to pull him back all morning.

Leaving his shirt where he had let it fall, Yuri stumbled unsurely down the meadow towards the fairy ring. He was almost relieved to see no sign of movement in it or anywhere near it. Suspecting the mechanism to be marking time below the ground he stepped into the ring believing he could jump aside at the slightest movement of the grass. But it was not the mechanism below that was waiting for him to arrive. Yuri was so taken with looking at what was happening inside the ring that he did not notice that an opaque curtain was suddenly drawn around the perimeter. He found himself wondering where the rest of the meadow had gone before he realised that it had completely enclosed him. The misty butterfly patterns that had reached out to him now engulfed him in their upward revolving spiral. The hand that had held him before now enclosed Yuri, plucking him with a traumatic jerk from his feet and whirling him with such frantic speed that he soon lost consciousness.

'Just how do Torrans manage to cope with these infernal tails?' complained Reniola. 'I think I prefer being a boulder after all.'

'They've got bones inside them attached to a nervous system you're supposed to operate,' Dax told her. 'You're not meant to keep treading on it, and if you do you're supposed to feel something that tells you it's painful.'

'Can't get the hang of nervous systems either. It's difficult to believe we developed from creatures that had them. Do you think we could swing from a branch with one of these appendages?'

'I doubt it. The Torrans only evolved tails as a form of ornament, and some of the bushier ones are grafted on after the originals have been worn out.'

'There is something strangely distracting in the thought that I am wearing somebody else's tail that has had more than two owners.'

'While you're developing a complex about your rear appendage you might like to give some thought to how you intend to rectify Moosevan's accretion equipment.'

Reniola was not enthusiastic about the reminder. 'Why can't *I* be Dax now? This Reniola creature's anatomy doesn't suit me at all.'

'Why don't you make your mind up?' snapped Dax in exasperation. 'It's too late now anyway. I've processed all her memory and reflexes so nothing would know me from the real thing.'

'Until you hit them with a nuclear punch.'

'That is something neither of us will use until it becomes absolutely necessary.'

'With these ears I wouldn't look forward to it either. They'd probably disintegrate before the rest of us.'

'We can always reassemble if that happens,' Dax told her, then stopped suddenly. 'Wait.'

'What's the matter?'

'Somebody else has arrived.'

'What? Another? I thought this galaxy was supposed to be running down.'

'It wasn't from this galaxy.'

'Oh no,' Reniola groaned. 'What is Moosevan up to? She's treating the gate like a plaything.'

'Moosevan only feels, does not see as we can. She has no mechanical knowledge so therefore does not understand the relevance of things that concern us. Her sensations are all, and she can only describe sensations.'

'Well, I hope she has a sensation telling her to put whoever it is back before they operate the net. Otherwise that means we'll have to deal with it.'

'Moosevan and her kind have strange ways, but they would not knowingly cause the death of anything living. We must deal with what we are here for. There will be time enough to check afterwards.'

'You speak for yourself,' complained Reniola. 'I've got to make a safe planet for her. I don't know why the confounded contraption should have stuck. It was only installed a thousand million years ago.'

They stopped their long strides to peer over a ridge at three suited figures below.

'Now what are they up to?' Reniola inquired.

'They are looking for the other new arrival. I'd better get down there and try to cut them off.'

'No chance on these clumsy leg things. You might be able to lure them away, but don't those creatures kill anything on sight and wonder what it was afterwards?'

'It'd be too awkward to transmute now. I'll have to make a run for it. You find the control point,' and without further ado she leapt away at a speed that the duplicate owner of her body would have found fur-raising.

Reniola scratched the unfamiliar muzzle that projected before her eyes and sloped off with a less energetic pace in the opposite direction.

Yuri clutched a handful of warm orange sand which ran through his fingers like mercury. As he looked about he found he was partly submerged in the powdery granules. They supported him like the caressing touch of the apparition which had snatched him away. He kept losing his balance as he tried to rise in search of some place to hide. Then he gave up in order to look at his bewildering surroundings. It did not take him long to realise that this was no place on Earth, or any planet near it. The red daylight sky, streaked with the rainbow-coloured remains of thousands of stars, told him that it was not even his own galaxy.

Yuri suddenly clutched his throat as he realised that he was breathing the familiar oxygen mixture humans could not do without, and wondered how long such an arrangement could last in these exotic surroundings. He was sure the purple-trunked trees with branches like chandeliers and flowers like carnivorous animals could not have been nurtured to maturity on such a thin mixture. Had he fallen anywhere else, Yuri knew he would probably have been smashed to pieces on the jagged rock outcrops or glazed marble sheets which surrounded the pool of orange sand. He was sure something had planned to break his fall and save him from suffocation long before he arrived.

Not knowing what he should be hiding from or where to turn to avoid it, Yuri dragged his sinking feet from the bed of sand to seek the cover of the trees. They looked dangerous enough in themselves, but he was sure their perfumed thoughts were strictly for the wind and other trees. He could see no other signs of life, like the animals or insects which he thought would have been necessary to fertilise the abundant vegetation that clung to every niche the ground allowed. This did not make him feel any easier. Perhaps this was a world where the vegetation browsed off the animals, and from the look of some of the specimens they lacked only the knives and forks to operate with.

Yuri struggled past twisted trunks and stems till he came to the edge of a high bank which fell sharply into the fast-flowing waters of a wide stream. He turned to push his way back through the vegetation only to find it had closed up to block his way. Then a long deep sigh echoed about him and he recognised the pervading perfume. Yuri was about to topple into the gushing water below when a wide dry path rose out of it to catch him before he could fall. Not knowing what had caused the freak tremor, but glad enough to be able to scramble away from the voice to the other side, Yuri fled as fast as the growth would let him.

Suddenly he reached an open space, and beyond that he could see a cluster of rocks. They were fused with vitrified minerals in a bizarre fashion which confused his limited comprehension of geology. Yuri ran his fingers over the glassy surfaces in wonderment and noticed how they seemed to collect the light of the yellow sun and radiate fluorescently. They lit the skin on his bare arms where the nettles had left their marks and slowly the irritation and angry swelling began to slip away. Though this did offer him some relief at the height of his traumatic experience, it did not last long. Soon a strange unreal whispering surrounded him.

He took a sudden bound on to the uneven rocks to try and escape it, but to his horror the rocks suddenly became smooth and he slithered back down to the sandy ground. Frantically he ran for the cover of the trees, but before he could reach them the ground itself had conspired with the rocks to rise into the sky and make a well from which he could not escape. Briefly, Yuri tried desperately to claw his way out of the trap, but soon realised it was no use.

He slumped down in the centre of the well and looked up to see the part of the sky which was still visible. Yuri imagined the walls would soon cave in to swallow him like a lion swallowing a gnat. He had quite forgotten the idea he had had about making contact with the unlikely entity, and was not very enthusiastic about its way of making contact with him. The soft whispering sigh echoed again about him.

'Creature . . .' it said, as it seeped into his thoughts, 'what are you . . .?'

Whatever this entity was, Yuri sensed that it was too large even for his much maligned intellect to comprehend and he crushed himself against the sand as though it could see him from the top of the well. Such a ploy was unable to fool it, and the words continued, 'What creature are you . . .?'

'Leave me alone,' Yuri eventually managed to reply, though whether it was with his tongue or mind he had no idea.

'What is the matter?' came the voice again.

'Let me out of here,' Yuri pleaded, and no sooner had he said the words than the walls began to shrink and he again found himself in the clearing with the trees on one side and the restored outcrop of rock on the other.

'You should not be alarmed,' the voice went on.

'Is there any rational reason for that statement?' Yuri asked in bewilderment.

The voice hesitated as though logic were something quite foreign to it, and eventually replied, 'I am Moosevan . . .'

If Yuri's hair did not stand on end quite naturally already it would certainly have done so at that admission. As Diana had refused to believe his zany fears, he had assumed her voice to be equally ridiculous. To discover that they were both right did nothing to improve his equilibrium.

'What is Moosevan?' he asked gingerly, something at the back of his mind telling him that he would have been better off without the answer.

'I am Moosevan,' the voice repeated as though that were the answer.

'Yes . . . . but what are you?' Yuri insisted, looking frantically about to see if the being were hiding behind some outcrop or tree.

'I am old . . .' Moosevan tried to rationalise. 'I am . . . Your touch pleases me . . .' she added as that was the most dominant thought in her mind.

'How old?'

'I must be half as old as this galaxy . . .' was the unusual reply.

Yuri looked up again at the sky scattered with the debris of so many stars and knew that that was very old. Normally he would not have sniffed at a show of affection coming from a mature woman, but one ninety thousand million years old was in his view taking things too far.

'That is very old . . .' gulped Yuri, 'but what do you look like?' he asked, suspecting that something so old was bound to be going off by now.

'I am here . . .' Moosevan insisted, wondering whether the belief she had about other creatures having eyes was in fact true.

'But I can't see you . . . Where am I supposed to look?'

At that, Moosevan gave a deep sigh. 'What are you called?' she asked in a languorous fashion, as though the knowledge of his name could heighten her contentment.

'Yuri,' he replied, not seeing any point in withholding it as she seemed to be in total command of everything else. He still thought he might try to dodge her attentions and rose in readiness to make another dash for what he thought to be freedom. 'Why won't you show yourself? Have you something to hide or do you think the sight of you would alarm me?'

'I would not alarm you, Yuri. Why should I alarm you?'

'I do not know,' said Yuri, 'but you have done very well so

far.' Then he made a successful sprint to the top of the rock outcrop and over the other side. Knowing he could not escape her, Moosevan let him go.

Congratulating himself on his ability to move so rapidly for someone fast approaching fifty, Yuri bounded over boulders and fought his way through trees before stopping to wonder where in this world he was going. He had no idea of where he was, apart from it being in a dying galaxy on the edge of the universe; or how he had got there, apart from it being through a children's fairy ring which was harbouring more than mushrooms. He sat down on the warm sand to rest.

It was not long before the inevitable voice of Moosevan caught up with him, asking, 'Are you tired, Yuri?'

'I am thinking.'

'What are you thinking, Yuri? Tell me.'

'I am thinking that as you do not want to show yourself to me, I should have nothing to do with you.' But his hand sank into the soft sand and the strange perfumed sensation rose through it to fill his body. As the engulfing caress of the creature encircled him he could hear Moosevan say, 'But I am here, Yuri . . . I am here.'

This time Yuri did not want to get up and run. The fear of contact with this exotic entity had left him, and a comfortably reassuring feeling had taken its place. Dancing ribbons of mist flickered round his body and mesmerised him into near sleep.

'I like your touch . . .' whispered Moosevan. 'You are not like anything I have touched before.'

Slowly Yuri felt himself sink to the soft sand where he lay gazing up at the sky of supernova remnants through a sparkling curtain of haze. Wondering why he should have been so panic-stricken, he let the waves of sensation flow over him like the undulations of a silken sea. Perhaps Moosevan was like the sea, fluid and reshaping. Perhaps she was like the sand he lay on, soft, warm and yielding. As he listened to her voice beneath, gently lulling him to sleep, Yuri cast his agile mind over all the things she could have been. Was she a phantom that lived in the magenta trees or like the vitreous substances permeated into the rocks? No, she could not have been those because her voice was everywhere, even beneath him.

Yuri's eyes suddenly snapped open in horror. He cast Moosevan's caresses aside as he leapt to his feet. Of course she was everywhere and he could not escape her. She was the planet. This was too much for even his broad mind to take. He bolted to the first gap he could see and on until his legs told him they could run no more and his reason had little to do but tell him that he could not escape.

There was a stretch of water ahead of him and had he managed to stagger to it, he would have seen it reach up in solid waves to break his fall. He chose instead to have his fall broken by the more unyielding pebbles Moosevan had not thought to adjust. He had not been lying there long before his attention was taken by two pairs of boots sculptured to the shape of large, splay, three-toed feet. This was something new. It may have had a considerable degree of nastiness about it, but it was still different.

Carefully Yuri raised his head to find himself looking up at two flat-headed green faces which peered back at him through polarised visors.

10

Eva stood looking thoughtfully at the slashed stinging nettles and discarded scythe and shirt. She could tell by the state of the weeds they had been attacked less than an hour before, and certainly not for the benefit of Daphne Trotter. The way that scythe had been used on the nettles indicated its wielder could have intended the same for the local harpy had she approached too closely to gloat. It did briefly cross Eva's mind that Yuri had perhaps concealed Daphne's dismembered body somewhere. There was no trace of bloodstains, and Yuri's arms, even holding the scythe, were too short to have hauled her from the horse. She dismissed the thought. She tucked a selection of his exercise books under her arm and walked thoughtfully back to her car parked out on the road leading to the museum. Coming along the road towards her were two shaggy individuals she had seen leading parties of the architecturally inquisitive and day-trippers round the grounds. Normally she would not have spoken unless they had shown some eagerness to be known to her, but she thought she might as well ask them as anyone else.

'Morning,' she said. 'Early lunch hour?'

'Yes,' said John, as Fran became apprehensive that a scientist should show interest in them. 'We've two parties coming at midday so we're having a break now. Looking for someone?'

'Yes . . . As a matter of fact I was. I don't suppose you've seen Mog, I mean Diana, anywhere about have you?'

'Di?' he asked as they stopped by the car. 'She's got the day off. Isn't she at home?'

Eva was irritated by John's ponderous manner, but she

replied politely enough, 'No, nor is Julia, and she's not with the looney Russian.'

Fran's mouth opened to make the standard protest at what could be taken as a racist comment, but John answered quickly, 'Can I take a message in case she drops in at the museum?'

'Not really . . . Thanks all the same. It's only something I thought she would be interested in.' They viewed her with ill-concealed curiosity, 'Something I dug out of some old records, about asteroids and alignments . . . and things. Probably nothing to worry about at all.'

'Not serious then?' probed Fran.

'No . . . it might not mean the end of the world,' she said as she opened the door of her car, 'if we're lucky.'

Had she realised where Diana was it might have dented even Eva's equilibrium. Having stood by the fairy ring long enough to make Moosevan understand that their contact should be much closer than from opposite sides of infinity, Diana had been allowed to enter that misty tunnel which had swallowed Yuri. No perfumed blanket of ardour for her, just an efficient snatch into emptiness and sudden jolt as she landed. Oddly, Diana could not remember anything in between, and fortunately knew nothing of the forces involved in making the trip possible. She did know that the moving porridge of prickly particles she had landed in had laddered her tights in three different places. Drawing in a lungful of air with surprise and annoyance, she parted her lips to bellow, 'Not funny, Moosevan!'

Moosevan immediately sensed her displeasure, even if she found her vocal rage incomprehensible. With a less passionate sigh than she might have used for Yuri, the larger of the females unrolled a thick mattress of gossamer seed heads and deposited that under her visitor instead. From being pricked all over, Diana was now coated with enough fluff to make her resemble a snow woman and sneezed uncontrollably as it was drawn up her nose.

'Cut it out, will you!' she spluttered in rage. 'Get me out of here, you lump of astral debris.'

Thoroughly disorientated, sneezing, and looking as though she had just escaped from an exploded mattress, Diana thankfully found solid ground under her feet. A light breeze picked the seeds from her one by one, while her thoughts churned in extreme annoyance. As the mental ferment subsided, the mellow appealing tones of Moosevan could be recognised asking, 'Are you well?'

Although her tongue was not going to make the reply, Diana had to spit out a mouthful of seeds before being able to think, 'That was not funny . . .'

'Funny?' queried Moosevan. 'What is funny?'

'Forget it . . . I don't suppose you do get to hear many good jokes out here.' Diana gave up and looked about her. She had found it difficult to believe Moosevan when she had described herself as just an ordinary planet. She was a planet all right, but certainly not ordinary. Something in the glowing reds and purple of the vegetation engulfing her was an accurate indicator of the planet's passion.

'You will not run away as well?' Moosevan inquired tentatively.

'In these shoes?' laughed Diana. 'Didn't I go through that mangle and fluff bath just to see you . . . or a bit of you anyway. As well as who?' Moosevan sighed heavily. 'Oh come on . . . who else have you snatched?' Before Moosevan was persuaded to reply she realised. 'Yuri . . . I should have known. What did you want him for?'

'He is pleasant to sense . . . His touch pleases me.'

'Oh, Jesus,' whispered Diana. 'A passionate planet.' Then to Moosevan, 'You can't have him, you know. Humans don't keep as long as planets.'

'When I have been driven out, I will cease to exist. I will replace him long before that happens. I will not let him come to harm.'

'But . . .'

'You have told me what would happen to your world if the parts of my new body were to reassemble.'

'I couldn't remember. I didn't realise I was aware of it,'

apologised Diana.

'You slept heavily. I took the message from deep in your mind,' said Moosevan.

'Thank God. I don't think I could have explained it while conscious.'

'I do not want to destroy your world. I no longer have the right to claim any part of it.'

'Are you sure about giving up the chance to stay alive? If there was any other way of keeping my world intact I would never ask it of you.'

'There is a way you can help me. If you can I will keep my promise.'

'What's that?' asked Diana, wondering what on earth she could do to help a planet.

'The small creature I took will not speak to me. I do not know why. I tried to reassure him, but he runs and runs . . .'

'Then leave him alone,' Diana told her.

'Leave him?' Moosevan replied in reluctance and disbelief.

'You sprang quite a surprise on him, but as he accepted your invitation into the ring it meant he was fascinated by you. He just didn't know his galactic girlfriend was going to turn out to be a planet. Give him time to get used to the idea. Keep quiet and see what he does.'

'But what will he do?' asked Moosevan.

'Forget it. There isn't time. Just believe me.'

'If you are right, I will do all I can to prevent those creatures from repairing the accretion machine which will destroy your world.'

'What creatures?' demanded Diana with a jolt more acute than the one she had arrived with.

'I do not know,' Moosevan replied carelessly, 'but I just felt one. It seemed to be tunnelling into my crust . . .' Then she lost interest. 'Tell me about this planet you live on. Has it a being like me?'

'There isn't time – this is urgent. Tell me about these creatures.'

'They are probably the Old Ones. They made the machine

that can help me pass from one body to another. Do not worry . . . I will not let them reach its control . . .'

'You don't sound sure.'

'Sure?' murmured Moosevan. 'So few things have bothered me for so long. Sure . . . urgent . . . What do these things mean?'

'They mean I am going to stay here until the last second to make sure these creatures are aware how urgent this situation is.'

'That would be dangerous,' Moosevan warned. 'You are so delicate . . .'

'Don't remind me of that!' snapped Diana.

'What is wrong?'

'Didn'f you feel my hot flushes?'

'Only once, and not since then. I don't think there is anything wrong with you now.'

Diana felt relieved. Even if she was going to be killed at any moment, the combat she had been having with her hormones could well be over. Whether this was something to be elated about under the circumstances she was not quite sure.

Reniola tried another explosive punch to get through to the next layer of rock Moosevan had used to conceal the precious equipment that had been installed millions of years ago for her preservation. She began to wonder if the creature wanted to be saved after all. The sheer walls were layered like the skin of an onion and grown of material so thick it was a wonder that Moosevan did not show some objection to her blasting her way through it.

. At last she came to a substantial cavity with walls glistening with sharp crystals. As she slithered through it she tripped and trod on her tail so many times she could have quite happily blasted that off as well. On and on through narrower and narrower passages the signal led her and she hoped Moosevan would not decide to breathe in at a crucial moment. Her natural vaporous form would have been no good in such a situation. It lacked fingers and the dimensional mortal reasoning crucial to

98

the matter in hand. So Reniola pressed awkwardly ahead until she came to another sheer wall of rock. It was so impregnable this had to be the place. The shock of the blast needed to get through it could easily irritate Moosevan and make her move violently enough to close every space and cavern beneath her surface. That would have been pretty inconvenient, but if the curious creature was to be preserved, the mechanism operating the accretion beam had to be mended. Vibration was out too. That could have shifted the crust without Moosevan's help and brought the roof down on the equipment as well as the engineer.

Reniola scratched her muzzle in frustration. It would be a simple matter for her to rectify the equipment, but the blasting artist was many miles upstairs pursuing some green creatures which were pursuing a very puzzled Yuri.

'Well, well, well. What is it?' asked Jannu in a way a spider might introduce itself to a fly as he bent forward to take a closer look at Yuri. 'I've never seen anything like it before.'

'It's not Torran is it?' pondered Tolt.

'No . . . I don't think its blood is yellow.'

'By the look of it, it might be congealed. Poke it and see if it moves.'

Jannu took the suggestion up and stabbed at Yuri's body with his foot. Something in the action told Yuri that these creatures were not the substance reasonable people were made of. He shrank back in a mixture of annoyance and terror, but took care that his hand closed round the largest pebble it could feel.

'Well, it obviously doesn't understand what we are saying,' sighed Tolt.

'Shall I kill it now then?' asked Jannu.

'Might as well. It can't be any use to us.'

'I suppose not,' Jannu said, taking out his weapon, but as the ground beneath them shuddered ominously, he went on, 'On the other hand . . . perhaps we should leave it alone. After all, we don't want her to get too upset before we leave here. We can let Kulp kill it. He's bound to be more efficient at that sort of thing than we are.'

'Oh, he's bound to be,' Jannu said. 'I wouldn't have the nerve to go and upset Moosevan like that. Would you?'

'Goodness no. If it's a friend of Moosevan's who are we to interfere?'

'What are you two gabbling about?' came Kulp's voice from a distance.

'We found the new arrival,' Tolt sang out.

'Well, stop messing about and kill it. We've got work to do,' Kulp ordered.

'Well . . . You're so much better at that sort of thing we thought you might like to do it.'

'Why start getting squeamish now?' demanded Kulp as he joined them. 'You've done enough killing in the past. Anyway, what is it?'

'I don't know. It won't answer,' said Tolt.

'Well, it can't be any use then,' snapped Kulp and pulled out his blaster.

'That's just what I said,' replied Tolt.

'What a coincidence,' sneered Kulp.

'Coincidence?'

'Yes, because that's just what I happen to think of you two as well. Stand over there with it so I don't waste any power when I kill all three of you.'

Tolt and Jannu exchanged looks that said they should have known better, and reluctantly lined up behind Yuri.

'I had planned a special treat for you, but circumstances and the opportunity cannot be missed so I'm afraid you will never know what it was.'

'Shame . . .' said Tolt, knowing quite well Kulp meant what he said. 'I don't suppose there would be any point in asking what brought about this rather drastic change of plan?'

'Oh . . . this and that. Small things like you offering to sell me out to the Mott.'

'Nothing more than that?' asked Jannu, knowing it would have been pointless to deny the charge because Kulp had probably added the memo to kill them both to his blueprints of the net. 'I hope the Mott won't take it too much to heart . . . or whatever they use in the place of one.'

'What possible use are you to the Mott, apart from blaster practice when they run out of living targets?' laughed Kulp. 'Don't worry. I'll deal with the commander and his whole species if necessary.'

Jannu and Tolt were able to take comfort in that statement because they sensed Kulp's arrogance had at long last brought him past the point of his normal self-importance. It was inevitable that the Mott would have decided views on who was the more superior.

'I hope you are going to kill our newly discovered specimen first,' said Tolt, 'just for friendship's sake.'

'Why not? What is a friend if you can't do him a favour?'

'Dead either way,' murmured Jannu, his brain racing to think of something Kulp had not taken into consideration.

But what Kulp had not taken into consideration was Yuri. As he raised his blaster to dispatch him where he sat, a large pebble hurled with more than David-like aggression struck the base of his visor and sent him reeling backwards. It had not been the atmosphere Kulp had wanted protection from so he had not locked the catch that held his helmet to the suit and it flew open to spring the helmet from his head before he could prevent it.

With as much amazement as Jannu and Tolt had delight, Yuri watched the loathsome green creature turn into a loathsome bright pink creature. Before the enraged colourful monster could rediscover where its quarry was, the three of them spread out: Yuri to dash for his life as soon as a clear run presented itself and Jannu and Tolt to jeer and mock the humiliated and unco-ordinated Kulp. Kulp was perhaps not so confused as they would have liked to have thought. He was able to raise his weapon and with remarkable accuracy shoot the catches from their helmets, which sprang from their heads in the same way. It was then that Jannu and Tolt realised the surprise Kulp had been about to spare them.

They looked at each other and saw that they had turned not only pink, but blue, magenta, yellow and orange as well. In fact there were few colours the stripes on their faces did not display. This was the last straw for Yuri and he turned on his heels to flee whether they were in a position to fire at him or not. Although he could hear the whirring volley of shots behind him, Yuri did not look back until he came to higher ground where he could take cover. His knees were no longer reliable after the experience, and he had to stop to recover the firmness in his joints and catch his breath. As he turned to look at the mêlée on the beach below, there suddenly appeared yet another intruder. Though elegant in comparison with the others, it was no less weird to his eyes. The unclothed parts of its body displayed a profusion of fur that would have made a Persian cat envious, and this did not exclude the long swishing tail. The muzzle would have given the creature a benign doggy sort of look if the eyes had not gleamed bright crimson like blazing coals. The three individuals with the complexion trouble still screamed strange noises at each other until the pink one turned and saw the newcomer. Yuri could tell by his actions that it was not a sociable meeting and his common sense told him to run.

'Dax!' screeched Kulp in rage so violent it was a wonder he did not glow red. Without waiting to introduce the arrival to Jannu or Tolt he fired his blaster. To his bewilderment and frustration the weapon had no effect on her. With the speed of the true fanatic, Kulp hurled his weapon at Dax and snatched Tolt's.

'Idiot!' shouted Jannu. 'Now run!' Tolt needed no further bidding. With the speed of two desperate hares the multi-striped engineers fled back along the route they had come. Kulp took no notice. He was filled with smouldering rage as he confronted the only creature to have not only outwitted, but humiliated him as well. He could see his life's ambition to destroy the Torran so near fulfilment even his own safety was a secondary matter. His cruel lips curled sadistically as he raised the weapon to again take aim at the fuzzy foe which looked down at him with an air of quizzical benignity.

'Having problems with your complexion, Kulp?' inquired Dax. 'You should keep out of the sun.'

Unable to stand her saying another word that could sear his glowing pink ears, Kulp pressed the trigger without stopping to wonder why he could understand her without the benefit of a translator. He was far more confused by the fact that Tolt's weapon seemed to be useless as well and the darts of venom filtered away into the atmosphere before they could reach their target.

'Now what have I said or done to upset you like that?' Dax asked sweetly. 'Anyone would think you were annoyed at something.'

Kulp was beyond words, and lunged towards her with some vague idea of wrapping his twelve fingers around her slender neck, but she was too quick for him. With a side step that her attacker would have needed three to equal she was standing on a gnarled tree trunk and still looking down at him with innocent concern. 'You shouldn't let things upset you like this,' Dax told him. 'After all . . . wouldn't the galaxy be a better place if we could all be friends?'

'Friends with a Torran!' roared Kulp as he realised that it was useless to try and kill her by any conventional means. 'I'd sooner befriend a Mott!'

'Oh, that would be taking things too far. I was only talking about the more reasonable species.'

'The Mott happen to rule this galaxy whether we like it or not,' Kulp snapped back as a more devious way of trapping her materialised in his one-track mind. 'So what are you doing here, my furry friend?'

'Me? I just heard that someone was going to drive the rightful owner out of its planet . . . And you know how us Torrans like to interfere when we have the chance.'

'So, that creature we found belongs to you? What was it? Some little distraction for us, perhaps?'

'Not especially,' replied Dax, annoyed that her suddenly acquired wealth of mortal knowledge could not tell her either.

'But you would be upset if any harm came to it, wouldn't you? You Torrans are soft like that.'

'It seemed from where I was standing it had no small power

to look after itself, so attempting to kill it might not concern me as much as you hope.'

'Well, let's put it to the test, shall we?' Kulp suggested. 'As you obviously aren't going to kill me, things would get a bit dull if there wasn't a victim of some sort.' He sprang off in the direction Yuri had taken.

Dax was not sure what to make of that. She wouldn't kill Kulp and Kulp couldn't kill her, so he was going to kill the intruder who neither of them knew anything about. The logic of incensed hatred was foreign to her, but the fact that he seemed to mean what he said made her decide to lope after him.

Unluckily for Yuri his age had managed to catch up with any surge of adrenalin his fright had given him, and he was reduced to staggering through the tangled vegetation. As nothing moved under or about him, he was at least thankful that Moosevan's passion seemed to have gone off the boil. Yuri's reason told him that affection for such an unlikely creature as a planet was not normal even for him, but his senses told him that her perfumed thoughts and misty fingers of sensation were something he could never have experienced in his own world. The more he thought about it and realised she had lost interest in him, the more he began to regret it. He could easily guess that Eva would have been unable to show the minutest fraction of such affection even if she thought him anything else but an encumbrance.

Gradually, Yuri's progress became slower and slower until he stopped completely and rested by a flower-coated boulder. He was so consumed in his own thoughts that he did not feel it move obligingly forward to shape itself to his spine. Yuri looked about him at the bewildering array of flowers, fruit, trees and rocks. It was as if Moosevan could not only design them, but rearrange them to fit whatever her strange tastes desired. If she wanted a mountain moved from one side of her world, he had no doubt she could do it, or even channel a whole sea across her surface in the same way. With that going on, it was hardly surprising mobile life-forms decided not to evolve there.

Slowly his contemplation turned to a longing for just one

small sign that she had forgiven him for running off. As though his wishes were about to be answered, Yuri heard a rustling in the branches a short distance away. He looked up to see the humourless pink expression of a fanatical Kulp.

11

'Use the boosters, use the boosters,' shouted Tolt, to which Jannu replied with equal vigour, 'Not yet, not yet. We'll be blown to bits if the beacons aren't aligned.'

'But I'm sure Kulp meant the boosters to be operated now. The robots can't hold the beacons in position without them.'

'Are you sure you two do know how to operate this net?' snarled the Mott. 'You'd better not make any mistakes.'

'We know, we know . . .' Jannu tried to reassure him while he endeavoured to recall the sequence in which the beacons had to be armed. 'We'll have to, because Kulp isn't likely to be finding his way back now.'

'I'm beginning to think this isn't such a good idea after all,' decided the Mott with enough malevolence to convince the two engineers that if they wanted to stay alive they would have to succeed in activating the space-distort net without any marked mishap.

'Wasn't there something we have to do to compensate for the collapsar?' Tolt whispered frantically to Jannu.

'The net has already compensated for it,' was the unhelpful reply.

'No . . .' hissed Tolt, 'I mean now, while we're still arming it?'

'Can't think of anything . . .' Jannu desperately tried to remember. 'If we don't get a move on, Kulp is bound to think of some dirty trick to escape from the planet.'

'Shall I start the countdown sequence now then? If we do think of anything we can always compensate for it afterwards.'

'At least this way we stand a chance of staying alive. Align the beacons.'

'All right,' said Tolt and began ordering his long-suffering robots to take their beacons to the correct positions.

'Ex 8 89 isn't responding,' Jannu informed him as he watched the remaining robot beacons leave the shute to glide across the sky to their certain destruction.

'Hang Ex 8 89. What difference is one unarmed terminal going to make?'

'I have a feeling we should know that,' answered Jannu, not liking to admit he was unable to understand all of Kulp's specifications. 'There isn't time to check without breaking the sequence.'

As Tolt and Jannu bumbled about in nervous confusion the Mott commander's four feet again became very agitated and seemed to do a little jig on the spot to stop him from galloping about the control room in rage. He was well aware of the procedure the Mott had for court martials. The main thing that made them different from any other species' was that the defendant was executed before the trial began. To their way of thinking this was more efficient, because they could always be found guilty on the grounds they had failed to give evidence in their defence. He knew. He had judged too many to suspect otherwise. It was not until now, when his life was on the line, that he fancied there could have been some error in the way they were conducted. He cursed to think he had allowed himself to be cornered into this situation by two soft-centred, addle-brained, treacherous green things who also appeared to have the disconcerting habit of acquiring multi-coloured stripes. Fortunately the stripes had disappeared rapidly before his one eye's limited discrimination became permanently offended. The only thing which prevented the Mott from airing his displeasure was the fact that his life was totally dependent on their muddled efforts to control something beyond their scope and very much further beyond his.

Having reached the spot where she had left Dax to pursue the three green creatures who were pursuing the strange intruder, Reniola stood still, trying to sense Dax's presence through the growing mist Moosevan had rolled across the landscape. Not overjoyed at Moosevan's timing for such an aesthetic feat, even though the mist hardly affected her sense of direction, Reniola made her way down to the pebble beach where it was evident that Dax had met up with the others. The scattered pebbles and discarded weapons told her that Dax had caught up with them, and the combatants had run off in different directions. Briefly stopping to wonder how Dax had managed to chase all of them at once without reverting to her natural form and probably in consequence forgotten what she was pursuing them for, Reniola located her trail and plodded on. The irritating mist began to lift and she sensed that Moosevan was being remarkably quiet for some reason. There was an element of the ominous in her mood as though she was waiting for the opportunity to pounce on something. Reniola just hoped that it was not going to be her and Dax. After all, they were trying to help the obstructive temperamental creature. If it were not for Torran enterprise and evolution they would not be there at all and her fate would have probably been sealed by the malfunctioning accretion equipment. What was causing the accretion beam to stall was beyond even the guess of Reniola's true self, since anything their engineers had perfected was unlikely to be anything but perfect.

Yuri felt a surge of terror rise from the pit of his stomach. It was bad enough to see one if those creatures green and behind a visor, but to see it pink and without one set up the sort of contradiction only a maleficent surrealist could paint.

A row of spiked fingers reached out towards him. He was so paralysed with fright he could only wince as they sank into his flesh and pulled him away from the boulder. Not daring to wonder why he had not been killed outright, Yuri let his captor lead him to the cover of some undergrowth. He was pushed to the ground and held there by the strength and steadiness of an educated gorilla. Although the language and movements of his captor were totally foreign to him, Yuri could tell by its premeditated manner that he was going to die anyway and he should be thankful he had been allowed to live that long. Although the creature carried no weapon it did not take him long to realise its powerful large hands could either throttle him or rip him apart in seconds depending on how gracious a mood it might be in.

The rustling movement from the trees indicated the arrival of the other oddity pursuing him. By this time Yuri had realised whose side he would prefer to be on if he had been given the choice. He managed to summon enough strength to let out a strangled shout of warning before Kulp smothered him more effectively with his free hand and dragged him into the clearing to hold his captive in front of him.

Dax was both mystified by Kulp's behaviour and baffled as to how she could do something about it without destroying his hostage. She knew if she walked away he would kill it as surely as she realised she was meant to stand there and watch him do it. Then it occurred to her that he was trying to provoke her into fighting hand to hand. She was too fast for him to catch but Kulp reckoned he was strong enough to do the same to her as he was doing to Yuri. Crude reasoning, not very elegant for Kulp, but effective in the absence of another solution.

Kulp's fingers seemed to turn into claws as they sank deeper into Yuri's flesh, making him gasp in pain. At the moment he thought his jugular vein was about to be ripped open, the brooding intelligence beneath them made its pounce. The ground below Yuri and Kulp suddenly ceased to be there, but before they could strike the bottom of the pit that had opened up, a shaft of rounded rock swung out from nowhere and batted Kulp high into the air. Before he could reach the ground again Yuri had been gently caught in a pool of soft sand and tumbled away from his descending tormentor. Moosevan could have so easily swatted Kulp back to the spaceship he had come from, but she seemed content to have Yuri safe. Even the furry creature seemed a little apprehensive about the sudden reaction from the planet, but seeing that Kulp had landed some distance away, bounded after him as though her sole interest was baiting him in some game with nonsensical rules.

Panting and weary, Yuri wondered how soon it would be before his next encounter with certain death. He stayed where Moosevan had put him in the hope she would contact him again. No movement or perfumed thoughts drifted up to greet him though, just the trudge, trudge, trudge of tired footsteps making their way through gravel and undergrowth towards him. Once again bracing himself for the inevitable encounter with alien terror Yuri saw another furry creature coming into view. This one was quite a bit plumper and more benevolent in appearance than the other. There was nothing wolfish in the way its eyes flashed when it spied him, and its rolling gait as it approached was anything but elegant.

'Hello,' said Reniola with a flicker of the nose that could have been a smile. 'I suppose you've just encountered a couple of unlikely characters pursuing each other? I don't know which was after which, but that's irrelevant.'

Yuri was amazed when the creature spoke, as it could not have had vocal cords designed to cope with any human dialect. Not wondering at Yuri's reluctance to reply, Reniola went on, 'Oh, you've got two languages, haven't you? Think I'll stick to this one if you don't mind. It's not much easier, but it's the one I picked up first.'

She sat down beside him. 'All this dashing about is beginning to get to me, you know. I'm sure these bodies were never designed for it. I only hope the original owner of this one doesn't ever lose the amount of weight from it that I have.'

Still mystified at the arrival of the amiable creature, Yuri pointed to the bushes and managed to utter, 'Your friend and other thing went that way.'

'I know,' said Reniola. 'But she's wearing me to a frazzle. They didn't make compensations for this sort of thing for when the Code was broken. It was all meant to be so straightforward, you see.'

Yuri found himself nodding his head in agreement for fear of opening his mouth to ask her what she was talking about. He had a feeling this was another thing he did not want to know.

'Now take those ridiculous Motts . . .' Then Reniola saw the bruises on his neck, and assuming he was as multiform as herself, went on, 'Easily damaged in that skin, aren't you?' She smoothed a furry hand over them and Yuri could feel the throbbing stop. 'They have the most incredible anatomy. Genetic engineers decided to take over when Nature didn't want anything more to do with them. Designed themselves an extra pair of legs and protruding teeth because they thought it would put the fear of demons into whoever they took it into their minds to invade. Did that all right, but now they have to eat through a straw and have trouble finding where it comes out the other end.' She looked at Yuri's numb expression. 'I can't say I've ever come across your type before, but from an on-the-spot judgement I would say you were a trifle overcome about something?'

'Things are getting on top of me . . .' Yuri managed to explain. 'I keep imagining this green thing which turns pink is wanting to kill me, and that this very large thing which is something like ninety thousand million years old is in love with me . . .'

'So?' inquired Reniola innocently, as though these things were a normal occurrence.

'This I would not worry about so much,' Yuri faltered, 'but I think I fall in love with it as well.'

'Oh, splendid. That might keep the old dear quiet for a little while. Can't work too well with all this thrashing and rolling about, you know.'

'But she is ninety thousand million years old.'

'Good age. She should go on for another third of that without any mishap. How old are you then?'

'Forty-eight or nine . . . I think . . .' he admitted guiltily.

'What? Thousand million?'

'No . . . years.'

'That's what I said. Thousand million years?'

'No . . . no . . . no . . .' Yuri insisted, shaking his grey frizzy hair, 'I mean forty-eight or nine years. How old are you?'

Reniola gave him a long studied look. 'Er . . . a hundred thousand million or so.'

'This I do not understand,' Yuri said, having no reason to doubt her.

'Well, it's quite simple, old thing . . .' Reniola was about to explain but hesitated; she couldn't think of anything that would make sense of the matter to her, let alone to the immature creature beside her. 'Perhaps our years run at different speeds.'

'That is probably it,' Yuri nodded sagely, not believing it for one second. 'What do you think I should do about this creature called Moosevan?'

'I don't see any harm in it myself,' said Reniola, scratching her muzzle. 'If she fancies you . . .'

'But now she will not speak to me.'

'Lover's tiff already? You'll have to humour her. Promised to someone else are you?'

'Oh yes. But my wife will not mind.'

'No?'

'She would not believe it. She believes nothing I say. Though she would probably insist we have a divorce if I told her I loved a female ninety thousand million years old.'

'Not a very understanding sort of creature, is she? As I see it, some life-forms are so blinkered they never think of investing in anything but what is immediate to their senses.'

'But what else is there to invest in?'

Reniola paused for a moment before replying, 'Ah . . . I see now. You're one of the first species types. That accounts for the age,' and she again scratched at her muzzle so vigorously a couple of whiskers came adrift. 'We were a good deal further up the tree when we opted out of this galaxy. What's left here is mostly supernova remnants and a general selection of genetic riff-raff.' She turned to him with a piercing gaze. 'You must still be in the birth/death league?'

'What other league is there?' asked Yuri in mystification.

'Oh . . . lots and lots . . . Most of the species left in this galaxy somehow managed to genetically engineer themselves back into the birth/death one. They thought my species one day launched itself into space to escape and fell off the edge of the universe.'

'Where did you go then?'

Again Reniola gave him a deep look with her crimson eyes and decided to be kind to him with half a truth.

'No universe has an edge to it, small strange one.'

'You mean space is not curved by gravitation, but infinite?'

'Not so much curved . . . as moving and crumpled.'

At that, Yuri's brain set to work to turn up his own comprehension of Reniola's model. When he thought he had grasped at least part of it he asked, 'Then you mean that space is being crumpled like so many pieces of paper, and where each crease makes contact with another there are two bodies of great density pinned together?'

'Something like that,' Reniola replied, assuming her comprehension of the stuff he was calling paper was the same as his.

'That means that matter can be sucked into one dense body and ejected through its mirror companion on to the other side of the crease. So each piece of paper is like a universe?'

'Or part of the same universe folded back on itself.'

'And that is how we could make a gateway to other parts of space?'

'It's the only way to get about,' Reniola assured him with the familiarity of experience. 'It's just a matter of knowing how to harness gravity. This galaxy is only sitting on a crease that has grown very large.'

'So there can be no end to universes? But what about the Big Bang?'

Reniola thought hard before replying, 'That must have been me falling off a rock.' She stretched her legs. 'Well, it's been nice chatting to you, but I must go now. Remember to keep away from that green thing that turned pink, won't you,' she advised him. 'Got to see what they're up to, I suppose. Cheerio.'

And before Yuri could reply, her long legs had carried her in the direction of her slim friend who enjoyed tormenting green creatures that turn pink.

His confusion changed to despondency, Yuri rose to dawdle from the patch of sand and wonder what he had wanted to do when he first stepped into the fairy ring. His thoughts on the matter were no longer real, though. Moosevan had grown a wall of imaginings about him that made fact fancy and fancy fact.

Careful to move in the opposite direction from the other eccentrics, Yuri passed through the curled, grey, satin grass of a plain spangled with bright red and yellow flowers. It seemed odd not to hear bird song and even the breeze was quiet as it brushed through the vegetation. Intently he listened for the sound of Moosevan's voice, but she was silent and keeping her passionate low whispers to herself. He tried to reason about how ridiculous it was to fall in love with a planet, and that nothing could ever come of it, but she had filled a void he had never realised was there before.

Sprays like strips of gold leaf floated from a slender branch above him, and waxy blooms descended to waft scent into his face as he passed, but they were no substitute for the perfumed misty caresses of Moosevan. Sensing that it was hopeless for him to expect to leave the planet, and that whatever he had come there for was a lost cause, Yuri sat in the grass that licked at his legs like cool flames. Stretching out and closing his eyes from the streaked sky and yellow sun's rays, he let his hand play with the friendly spiralling blades of grass. Filled with sweet regret he heard his lips whisper, 'Moosevan . . .'

Strange soft wisps of mist flowed across his body to shroud him in distinctive perfume. Caressed by familiar fingers, Yuri heard Moosevan's gentle voice.

'Yuri . . . You are sorry?'

'Yes. I didn't understand . . . You forgive me?'

'I am not angry. There is not much time for us now.'

'But the creature I spoke to said you had only lived two thirds of your span,' protested Yuri. Another thought crossed his mind. 'You mean *I* will not live much longer?'

'You will live to your natural old age but I will soon have to pass from this planet. It is like a body to me and without it my spirit cannot survive long enough to reach another shell.'

'But why? Why?'

Moosevan sighed again. 'I am not good at understanding these things. The ways of some creatures are very strange to me. I know that surrounding me they have made a net that will distort the very space I sit in. I understand that this distortion will be so great that it will drive me out . . . like a spirit from its body.'

'But they must be stopped,' insisted Yuri, feeling at that moment that he could have done it himself.

'I have lived long. I do not kill other creatures, and this is what I would have to do to stop them.'

'Let me do it.'

'You are foolish. I would not let you kill for me.'

'But there must be a way out. I can't bear the thought of you dying.'

'It does not matter that much to me. I just wanted to touch you once more before it happened.'

'But what are those tall furry creatures doing here if it isn't to save you?'

'They are being foolish as well. They are great intelligences even older than myself, but they do not know what I have been told.'

'What is that?' asked Yuri, and then he found he was listening to the very story he had worked out for himself.

'When those great intelligences passed from this galaxy by developing cosmic forms, they left an escape route for every planet creature like myself in this galaxy. We could not adapt as they could, and they realised the time would come when evolution retrogressed and produced species which would soon turn their greedy eyes to our fertile worlds. Knowing what the nature of these creatures would be they were aware that sooner or later they would try to drive us from our bodies and let us perish in space. So they built gateways into other galaxies across the universe. Through them we were able to slough enough material from ourselves to form new ones when the time came. In this material they put machines to tell the pieces how to come together when the time came. Being the substance of our own bodies we could rearrange its elements to suit our needs after it had accreted.'

'But why didn't they form whole planets to begin with?'

'Because they would have been near enough to a sun and with enough elements to form life, and what species would fancy living on a planet that they are totally at the mercy of?'

'I see.'

'I did send a signal to the machine on the other side of the gate, but it was intercepted,' Moosevan went on. 'I was told that the densest part of the new planet was embedded in another world when it was accreting material. This planet now has life, and would be smashed apart if I were to operate the machine.'

'That is true. That is the planet I come from. If that machine should operate and form your world it would destroy mine.'

'But it will not, I have made the accretion beam cease to function so there will be nothing for me to pass to once I have left this planet.'

'But that cannot be,' protested Yuri. 'You cannot die like that.'

'I must. If those two creatures from the Old Ones manage to reach the control inside my crust they will undoubtedly make the machine function whatever I try to do about it. They must not reach it if you are to live.'

'But if you die I don't want to live.'

'You hardly have any life at all as it is, but I will not let you die. You must return to your own planet soon.'

'But surely they could stop the other creatures instead?' asked Yuri in desperation.

'But they must not be aware of who they are. If species like the Mott know the Old Ones have returned and the Code has been broken, they would exterminate all those people they suspect were responsible. It is a very small price to pay. You must not take this so seriously. You will think it just a dream when you are back in your own world.'

'It will always be a nightmare. Won't you try to think of a way to save yourself just for me?'

'It is just for you and your kind that I will not.'

'Let me stay . . .' pleaded Yuri, 'I have nothing much to go back for.'

'I will let nothing harm you, Yuri. You have had enough confusion and frightening experiences for such a short life.'

'You will send me back through that black hole?' Yuri asked as he realised the meaning of the black disc in the sky. He had not thought of it as such before, even though it reflected no light, because it had no effect on the planet it circled like a moon, but Moosevan's story convinced him.

'I will send you back through the gate the Old Ones built and you will return to your own world,' Moosevan reassured him.

'But to go through that thing would crush me out of existence.'

'You came through its beam, so there is no reason why you should not return the same way. We should not argue like this. You are a strange one to need to argue so much.'

'I have to squeeze all my arguments into a much shorter space of time than you do. I will not argue any more if you do not want.'

'You must rest now,' Moosevan whispered, and the soft perfumed veil was once again drawn over Yuri's thoughts.

12

Daphne faced the grave Mr Turner and assured him, 'But he's really quite tame, just looks a bit on the ferocious side.'

'That's as may be,' replied Mr Turner, who knew better than to contradict her: his farm was rented from her family. 'But I'm glad I had those fences seen to last winter. He looks a ferocious brute to me, even though you say he isn't. I can't say I'm happy about it because children expect to play in that meadow.'

'But you own the land,' snapped Daphne. 'You might as well have some profit out of it instead of letting it permanently lie fallow.'

'But I'm thinking about the other people in the village who've come to regard it as a right of way,' moaned Mr Turner. 'I've got no right to stop that Russian fellow with the telescope leaving his cottage.'

'You've got every right. He can run fast enough, and so can anyone else who wants to visit him. The person who bought the lease on that cottage should have remembered to buy a right of way as well.'

Mr Turner knew the consequences of trying to divert Daphne's mind from what it was set on, and leant on the sturdy fence to watch the massive black beast making charges at phantom cloaks. 'If he's harmless I'm the sugar plum fairy,' he thought to himself as the bull's sharp hooves ploughed up buttercups and daisies that had been growing quite happily there for years. He racked his brain desperately for some solution that would let him off being party to some poor creature's goring. This bull was obviously being kept from the performance uppermost in its mind. Being confined without a girlfriend was hardly going to sweeten its temper.

'Magnificent creature,' sighed Daphne, her ample chest and body swelling with pride despite the corsets they had been crushed into.

'Then why put it to grass, Mrs Trotter?' Mr Turner asked in mystification.

'I want it to be built up, Mr Turner,' Daphne lied.

'If that beast is built up any more it'll be too heavy to serve an elephant,' Mr Turner informed her, but she paid scant regard, preferring to watch the black brute make practice charges at Yuri's gate as it swung in the breeze.

Realising there was nothing legal or illegal he could do about it, Mr Turner resolved to pay a visit to the parish church for the first time in years and see the vicar to make his peace with God just in case. Climbing wearily into his battered land rover, he drove off to go and count sheep out of the dip.

The freighter released its load of beacons and slipped away from the range of the space-distort net. This was vital as the device would effectively twist anything within its range inside out and back again . . . if the sequence and all else Jannu and Tolt had guessed at was right. They had doubts about it, but were keeping it to themselves. The Mott commander had the same doubts gnawing at his badly designed bowels. Despite his misgivings, the four-legged gentleman insisted on remaining in the blasting zone with them on board Kulp's powerful ship. Kulp had prepared everything to suit his efficient way of working, and this alone effectively confused his two partners.

'Right trajectory of the planet won't be long now,' Tolt informed the others. 'The sun must be directly behind it and the collapsar at its side.'

'Where does it say that?' demanded Jannu.

'On Kulp's sequence list.'

'If he had a sequence list made out all the while, what have we been doing guessing at everything?'

'I didn't think we could trust it. He might have just left it for us to find in case we dumped him, and kept the sequence in his head. He's intelligent enough to remember it.'

'Then why trust it now?' hissed Jannu out of the Mott's translator's hearing.

'Because I have this feeling of desperation overtaking me and I've got to trust something,' he hissed back. 'Got any better suggestions?'

'No, only don't do anything to make the Mott more nervous than he is. He keeps passing wind and it is very unpleasant.'

Bearing that in mind Tolt carefully started to arm the terminals. The one on the planet had already been armed by Kulp and both of them knew enough to realise that not even he could have disarmed it. Still nursing fears that Kulp might find some way of clambering back to the control ship, Tolt gradually speeded the dangerous process up until Jannu reminded him, 'Take it easy. Remember to give us enough time to get out of here.'

'Now Ea 8 88 won't respond,' hissed Tolt petulantly.

'It's probably a conspiracy with Ex 8 89.'

'It's not funny!' Tolt snapped. 'You should have checked their maintenance on the way here.'

'That was your job as well.'

'It was not. You told me you were going to check them. I was plotting the route . . .'

The Mott was lost for words at their sudden display of petulance, and weighed up the pros and cons of killing them then and there. But however temperamental these two were, they knew more about the space-distort net than he did. In fact, all the glowing intellects in the vicinity were on the planet's surface. Unfortunately not many of them were engaged in profound thoughts that might have improved the situation.

Perched on the edge of a cliff behind a boulder just light enough for him to move and heavy enough to crush a Torran, Kulp waited with fanatical patience for his prey to lope past. With unerring precision Kulp's immaculate sense of timing sent the heavenly gift tumbling down to meet Dax at the exact

120

instant she was directly beneath. Kulp was already celebrating so he did not bother to look over the edge of the cliff to see the result of his handiwork right away, preferring to relish the moment like old brandy. When his three-toed feet had stopped springing him up and down in delight, Kulp's pink features poked themselves over the edge to savour the sight of a squashed Dax. And with injured innocence, Dax stood amongst the remains of the shattered boulder, looking back up at her attacker with something resembling pity for his mental condition.

Logic had always been Kulp's strong point, and this last incident had no place in it. He had hit her. He could not have missed, and when the furry creature called up to him, 'Look . . . I know you're enjoying yourself, but I really can't stop to play any more,' he launched himself from the cliff to see if he could do what the boulder had not.

Dax stepped aside so he could break his fall on the shattered boulder, then looked down at the breathless body. 'There's no need to take it so badly. I've got to get back now. Time must be getting short.'

The genetic engineers had designed his bones to be as strong as steel, but Kulp felt his internal organs judder about inside him and his brain cells slop around in his skull. He hauled himself to his feet wondering whether his increasing insanity would be contagious to the self-sure Torran. Something in that addled soup of his mind must have told him that this Dax was not the one he had known and loved to hate. Nevertheless, this one he could take satisfaction in despising even more.

'I suppose you might be a little happier if you were to become your normal colour again?'

Kulp was not sure what she had said at first. He was listening to his own thoughts preparing her destruction.

'Would you calm down if you were that indelicate shade of green again?'

Kulp could hardly believe his ears. Hating this creature was obviously getting him nowhere except painfully dented. Then some glimmer of light snapped open a part of his brain that had never functioned before. It had been deliberately left undeveloped by the genetic engineers for fear of it weakening the species. Could he be the first of his kind for millions of years to hear its faint cry? 'Why bother to hate?' it asked. 'Isn't it a waste of time?' Kulp was not able to answer it right away as the idea was such a novelty. He above all others had managed to control his emotions with cool malice, and any sentiments managing to escape through the veneer had more to do with greed than benevolence. This surely could not be the only emotion available to an intellect such as his.

Dax's furry hand flicked swiftly in front of his pink face and across his body, then he sensed the tickle of change go through him. He raised his hands as she lowered hers and saw that they had reverted back to their normal green. He pounced on the nearest rock with a vein of reflecting crystal running through it, managing to glimpse enough to see that his face was its normal ugly colour. Kulp's immediate reaction was to wonder where the catch was, but it was soon evident that a creature with that sort of power did not need to be devious like him. Then the thought of thoughts filtered through his mind. Should he or should he not cease being Kulp the unspeakable and become Kulp the reasonable?

The enormity of his own potential drove the green superbeing into assessing those avenues which his mind had always shuttered off before. There, twinkling like new star systems, hung clusters of tempting invitations. They begged him to contrive the execrable in the name of that mystic cult of justice the Torrans had adopted. If they could do outrageous things in the name of justice and be revered for it, why not he? Thanks to the Mott advance he was wealthy enough now to afford the luxury of morals. Kulp knew he had no hope of transforming into anything like one of the ethereally innocent creatures which lived in lace webs, were born and died in a puff of vapour, lived off clean thoughts, and minded their business so well few had ever seen one. So he resolved to put his evil ideas to a good use. What was good and evil if not a matter of opinion anyway? One just made a quicker return than the other.

With the change of mind came a flutter of euphoria which substituted for the rapturous elation most others would have experienced. Kulp liked the sensation. Reassured that there was no dishonour in capitulating to any creature a thousand times more menacing than himself, Kulp decided he could also afford the luxury of staying alive while the offer still stood.

His returning sense told him that these creatures were not to be trifled with and deceived like the usual run of galaxy hoi polloi. They were so potentially dangerous and indestructible he would have to control any latent urge to betray them should it ever cross his mind. But, if he did not show some signs of moderate behaviour, he would soon end up spinning in space like the doomed Moosevan.

Although she was in a hurry to return to a more important matter, Dax hesitated and assessed the changing thoughts of Kulp. If they revolved sufficiently to her way of seeing things he might well be worth recruiting. For a greedy, ruthless, genetically manipulated specimen, he did have a remarkably useful brain. If its encounter with her had not left it in a state of irreversible cataplectic damage, it might well prove invaluable.

'Do you want to join your friends now?' Dax asked, to measure his reaction.

'I'd only have to kill them if I did, and that would be a waste of energy.'

'Would you like to kill them?'

'No need. They don't know enough about the net to operate it. They're bound to kill themselves when they try.'

That was half way to what Dax wanted to hear, and she lifted a long finger to caution him. 'With us there is no deceit. While you are taking into consideration the benefits of being trustworthy, remember that.'

'All right,' Kulp agreed. 'What do you want me to do?'

'You must realign the beacons and arm the terminals in their correct sequence,' Dax told him. His bottom jaw dropped. 'If they are fired in the way your friends have arranged they will not only destroy this planet, but themselves as well.'

'I'd have to kill them to get near though,' protested Kulp.

'That will not be necessary. But as they are about to trigger the system we will have to move quickly.'

Still puzzled, but not ungrateful for being given the chance to realise the potential tucked secretly away in his brain for so many years, Kulp complied with her suggestion and listened intently to her instructions.

Having retreated to what they thought would be the safety of the Mott monitoring station, Tolt and Jannu installed the firing mechanism for the net. Unable to forget his concern for Mott property, even under those ringlet-raising conditions, the Mott commander looked worried.

'Damage that console and it'll be deducted from the payment you get,' he whined, as he saw them levering pieces of his observation chamber away to reach the mechanics beneath it; it did not improve his mood that Jannu had managed to talk his own service robots into helping them, and anger briefly blotted out the awareness of their danger.

'I can remember where everything goes,' Tolt assured him.

'It's a pity you couldn't do the same for the net,' retorted the Mott. 'If this goes wrong you know what will happen, don't you?'

'I know, I know,' sighed Jannu. 'We won't get the Mott award for practical engineering.'

'We've got to do some damage to the console to install the firing gadget,' explained Tolt. 'Every second we spend installing this means we're not able to monitor the beacons. We can't reconnect the scanner until we've finished. You wouldn't have liked to stay in Kulp's ship and discover some booby trap in the middle of firing, would you?'

At last the botching and bumbling about was completed and Tolt activated the monitor's scanner which sat in a pile of materials that had once been the Mott's console.

'Great, great,' sang out Jannu in uncharacteristic delight. 'Ex 8 89 and Ea 8 88 have aligned themselves.'

'That was lucky,' said Tolt.

They were both incompetent enough to take the unlikely

occurrence as being more fortuitous than sinister.

'We must have got it right after all,' Jannu went on. 'The sequence lights are checking out.'

At that they heard a gasp of relief coming from both ends of the Mott commander who had been thinking more of his court martial than a closer death.

'Luck must finally have paid us a visit,' Tolt said. 'Shall we need to pull Kulp's ship out of range now?'

'Not now we know things are going to work out,' replied Jannu. 'We may not have to try and make a run for it after all,' he added in a low whisper.

13

'What do you mean you can't get through?' demanded Dax.

'She keeps making barriers,' Reniola explained. 'I thought she would have wanted us to save her, but it wouldn't surprise me if she had made the control malfunction in the first place.'

'What would she want to do that for?'

'Well. There must be some things even we don't know.'

'Moosevan is going to be saved whether she likes it or not,' Dax said firmly. 'Once we get through to the control equipment she'll have no choice in the matter. Everything will be ruined if she isn't.'

'Well, she may not have tried to trip us up or bury us so far, but it doesn't seem as though she's going to speak to us either.'

'Of all the planet dwellers the Mott could have chosen, they had to pick this one. We can't wait around any more. Kulp is due to trigger the net with the others pretty soon.'

'You are sure we can trust him?' asked Reniola.

'Now his latent conscience cells have been activated there will be no problems, even though he's still learning to use them. In the Olmuke they had been artificially suppressed so if any of them did happen to have a good side to their nature they would never have known about it.' She turned on her heels to usher her companion back. 'Where is the control anyway?'

'A long way down. Couldn't you have thought of more suitable bodies to get into than these?'

'No. We need fingers and legs and a large enough brain to hold the information. Stop grousing, can't you?'

'I don't like bodies,' Reniola persisted, leading Dax to where she thought she had blasted an entrance into Moosevan's crust. 'They're uncomfortable, need too much maintenance and can hurt if they don't get it.'

'You wanted that one,' Dax reminded her.

'Only because it looked more comfortable. Someone might have told us what to expect.'

'Who would have known anything about the life here if the Torrans hadn't broken the code? Who would have thought anyone would have evolved sufficiently even to try?'

'It's going to be one heck of a job evacuating this place when the time comes. We've got to find somewhere to put them . . . and all within a million years or so.'

'Let's finish this job first,' Dax advised her. 'We can worry about taking the Mott's little toys from them after that.' She stopped before the sheer wall of solid rock Reniola's path led them to. 'Now where's the entrance?'

Reniola looked up at the barrier with a mixture of amazement and pique before saying, 'Moosevan has filled it in.'

'That did occur to me as an explanation,' said Dax as she drew a matchbox-sized instrument from behind one of her large furry ears. 'If that's her attitude she certainly won't enjoy this very much.' Reniola twitched her nose and flinched as a shaft of concentrated light hit the rock face. At first only slithers of its surface spun away to be filled in just as rapidly, but Dax increased and localised the beam on one spot. She began to bore a way through too rapidly for Moosevan to continue sabotaging their work.

In the gloom, their luminous eyes looked down into the abyss of a fault that had not been there on Reniola's first journey. Being solid may have come in handy in other ways, but if either of them fell to the bottom, it would have taken more time than they had to clamber back up.

'Get ready to jump,' Dax told Reniola, and sprang across the void before she had time to hear the inevitable complaint.

Reniola was far from keen, so Dax shouted, 'You'll have to do it. I can't fix the control without you.'

Reniola pondered why, after so many years of existence, she

had not taken provision against such an eventuality as having to jump across an abyss in somebody else's skin. Finding no adequate answer, she took a deep breath and launched her plump body in the direction Dax had taken. At long last she discovered a real use for that long furry tail she thought such a nuisance: as her grip slithered away from the hold she had on the crumbling rock Dax seized the swishing appendage and swung her from the ledge and across the abyss again to safety.

'I thought Moosevan never entertained ideas of murder?' Reniola complained, retrieving her stretched tail from Dax's grip.

'She probably knows we can't be killed. She's pitting her strength against our wits.'

'This is a very elaborate way to try and commit suicide, though. There must be more to it than that?'

'Why not ask her?'

'It's easier blasting holes through rock than trying to get her to say something to us. I suppose as temporary mortals we should feel aggrieved by this unco-operative attitude?'

'The only thing I feel at the moment is impending doom for this mission if we can't get her to pass through the gate to her new body.'

'Perhaps she doesn't like the decor?'

'It hasn't even been constructed yet. That's what you are supposed to be down here to rectify.'

'I suppose I could add a few extras for her. Like a multi-banked cloud system she could blow about a bit, or self-draining oceans . . . She doesn't have that much water on this one . . . or even that little creature she's taken a fancy to . . .'

'If she isn't going to consult with us on the matter, it'd all be guesswork,' Dax reminded her. 'You might as well throw in half a dozen satellites she can juggle with for all the difference it'll make to her stubbornness.' She hesitated. 'What little creature she's taken a fancy to?'

'The one Kulp and his friends were going to operate on,' Reniola told her impatiently.

'Of course . . . She was quite upset when Kulp was going to throttle it.'

'Nothing much could have come of it though. The age difference would have been a bit on the uncomfortable side.'

'Really . . . These planet creatures are supposed to live more from their memories than from direct experience, so I suppose he could have been kept alive for her in a sense after he was dead.'

'I suppose so, I suppose so. I only hope she remembers to put him back where he came from in time.'

'Oh, she probably will,' replied Dax. 'It's us she seems to want to be shot of . . . Look out!'

From somewhere in the high ceiling of the cavern a cascade of jagged stalactites rained down so rapidly on them it combed their fur.

'I can do without those sorts of trimmings,' said Reniola, taking cover.

'Don't be daft. They can't harm us.'

'Then why make me jump like that?' protested Reniola, crawling from the cleft she had squeezed herself into.

'Must be something to do with these mortal reflexes. I seem to have as much trouble with them as you do with your tail.'

'Let's turn into a couple of armour-plated shale crawlers. I once heard they have nerves of pure diamond.'

'They have. They also have intellects much lower than that of solid rock and we would probably spend the rest of that incarnation wondering what we were doing in here. Now stop moaning and come on.'

It was inevitable they should come to the layers of rock Reniola was sure she had already blasted through, but when they reached their destination and the control signal could be heard, a new addition to the defences was discovered.

'Where are we?' murmured Dax in bewilderment.

'This was never here before,' Reniola assured her. 'She surely couldn't have done this in so short a time.'

'She certainly must be determined if she did,' said Dax, scratching her nose in uncharacteristic inelegance.

As far as they could see stretched the wall of a dome made up of nothing but large clumps of the hardest crystals ever to grow. Dax could not measure their depth, but sensed that they were still growing as she watched: layer upon layer to encase the control equipment away from their reach.

'How long have we got now?' asked Reniola, not doubting Dax's ability to break through the ambitious chemical reaction, but wondering if she had the time.

'Not long.' Dax reset her cutting beam. 'Are you sure the control's behind that?'

'Positive.'

Without another word, Dax aimed the beam at the nearest cluster of crystals which sparkled defiance at her. At first it seemed as though they were growing again as fast as she cut them, then without warning she switched her position and aimed her cutter at another spot. Not able to compensate in time, Moosevan gave her the chance to break through. Soon the disintegrating surface flowed past their feet in streams like glassy syrup. The streams became rivulets, and eventually their flow suddenly ceased as the beam penetrated the control chamber and lit it up in a sudden flash of light.

The massive chamber was more or less in the state it had been left in many millions of years previously, and the control equipment to operate the linking of the planetoids still sat in its transparent cocoon like an idol on a plinth. It winked and twinkled with the rotating lights that had been operating since its construction. Dax, not being given to intuitive twinges, missed the obvious presence which Reniola immediately spotted. There was something standing in the shadow of the equipment. It was not close enough to be illuminated, and too far behind it to be seen clearly, but it was obviously alive. Dax immediately stopped trying to break through the casing of the equipment. Not knowing what to expect, and even a little put out by the fact that it had taken two intelligences like themselves so long to get so far, she called out, 'Who's there?'

The figure slowly began to move as though not understanding what she had said, but being able to guess the gist of it. As it walked into the light of the equipment, Dax and Reniola immediately sensed something disturbing about the stranger. It did not take Reniola long to be able to ask it in its own language, 'What are you doing here?'

'Delivering a message,' was the reply.

'Why like this?' Dax managed to inquire as she recovered from her surprise.

'Moosevan is stubborn,' the intruder replied. 'She insisted on doing things her way. My message is the same as hers, only I intend to make you understand it.'

'What is it then?' asked Reniola, mystified as to why the visitor could not have used less dramatic a means of delivering it.

'You must not activate the signal which will accrete the new planet for her. The major portion of its mass is inside a world which has many life-forms of its own.'

'That's all we need,' Dax sighed, as her knees at last decided to buckle and deposit her narrow backside on the most convenient rock. 'That's why she didn't want to go.'

'It figures,' replied Reniola. 'I'll just run a test through the gate and check.'

'It's got to be the truth,' Dax told her. 'If there wasn't a planet there, where would she be getting her boyfriends and messengers from?'

'I didn't think of that,' Reniola confessed, feeling the discomfort of an embarrassed blush beneath her fur. 'I wonder why it never occurred to us?'

'Perhaps there's no difference between knowing everything and seeing nothing. We'll have to be more careful in future.'

'So now what?' asked Reniola. 'Goodbye Moosevan?'

'No . . .' protested Dax. 'There has to be a way out of this.'

'Well, don't take the one that blasts a hole in my planet,' Diana warned, waving her handbag in agitation at them. 'I would like to go back there when this party's over.'

'We'll think of something, we'll think of something,' Dax tried to reassure her, racking her Torran brain. 'Only it will have to be quick.'

Reniola seemed to be spending an uncomfortable amount of time rummaging about in the ancient equipment, pulling out bits and pieces of this and that, and putting them back in a different order. Intrigued and suspicious as to what she could be up to, Diana demanded, 'What's your friend doing?'

'She's just checking things out. Moosevan's been interfering with the equipment.'

'As long as she doesn't mend it,' Diana threatened, though not quite aware of what she was going to do about it if they decided not to listen to her.

'Not much time now . . .' sighed Dax. 'Hadn't you better be getting back?'

'There is little point in me getting back to where I came from if my planet is going to be blasted into small pieces across its solar system as soon as I arrive.'

'But it won't be,' protested Dax.

'What's that?' asked Diana in alarm as a deep shuddering pervaded the chamber.

'It's started. Think of something.'

'Hope Kulp takes his time over it,' Reniola called back over her shoulder.

'Kulp may be reformed,' Dax reminded her, 'but that doesn't mean it's affected his efficiency.' She turned to Diana. 'How did you get here?'

'I'm not telling you, and I'm not moving.'

'Moosevan could only have brought you through the gate. What's happening to the gate, Reniola?' Dax demanded, as the shuddering became worse and rocks were dislodged and flung about.

'All in good time, all in good time . . .' Reniola said soothingly, as though she was oblivious of the beacons triggering their distorting web.

'We don't have time,' Dax protested, but Reniola continued to coolly poke and probe about the equipment, totally immersed in what she was doing.

Aware that Diana did not have the same degree of indestructibility as themselves, Dax hustled her to the shelter of the plinth so she only underwent the minor risk of being struck by the bits and pieces Reniola was rearranging inside it. The shuddering grew and grew, and larger and larger rocks were shifted to crash to the floor of the chamber.

'Assuming we ever think of anything which is liable to suit all of us, and the gate is still operating,' Dax asked Diana, 'where would you like us to drop you off?'

'Assuming my planet isn't blown to smithereens, I would prefer it to be somewhere on that.'

'No, no, no. I meant, whereabouts on your planet?'

'You mean I have a choice?' Diana asked in amazement. Briefly she considered a trip to the French Riviera, but remembered she would never get back in time to make Julia's tea.

'Oh yes,' Dax assured her as she just managed to catch a small rock before it hit Diana and handed it to her as a souvenir. 'Moosevan could only have managed to take people from one particular point selected by the control equipment, but she could put them down anywhere on her surface. Assuming the planet isn't turned inside out before the equipment is mended, Reniola will make the system open-ended. The scope would have been wide enough to get Moosevan herself through.'

Diana was about to nod her head in counterfeit understanding, when Reniola sang out amidst the descending pieces of the chamber's ceiling. 'All ready now. Where does our friend want to go?'

'What do you mean? All ready?'

'While you two were jabbering on, I not only thought of a solution, but have adjusted the equipment to try and make it work.' Reniola shrugged. 'Don't know if it will, of course, but whether it does or doesn't, it'll be easier than walking.'

Dax's crimson eyes looked into Diana's wide ones. They both knew they had to accept Reniola's solution. They could worry about what it was later.

14

After recovering from having Dax reduce his body to molecules then fire them into his ship, Kulp sat quiet and motionless as a deep green pool. He patiently waited for the bumbling trio in the Mott monitoring station to trigger what they thought would be the signal to activate the space-distort net. It did not need his greater intellect to tell him that in their simplicity they had not anticipated his seemingly miraculous return to his ship.

Kulp found it hard to take instructions from creatures who could change shape easier than he could change colour, but knew that he was not only on the right side now, but the winning one. He wondered briefly how Tolt and Jannu would react to his new way of looking at an ugly galaxy, and was slightly perturbed to find that he could not guess. If greed and fear had not overtaken them, perhaps they too could have released that small suppressed area of the brain that allowed a glimpse of sparkling honesty. Not knowing what honesty was, let alone that it sparkled, the experience might have proved too much for their already confused minds.

Kulp realigned the beacons and persuaded the two errant robots to take theirs to the right positions before Tolt had fitted the firing mechanism in the Mott's observation chamber. He then reconnected the firing command and monitored their signal to make sure his synchronised with theirs. He expected there to be some delay as they quibbled about how safe it was and who was to do the dirty deed, so he waited, cat-like, to pounce as soon as the signal arrived. Once he had that, things would be completely out of their incompetent control, and it mattered little whether they discovered his presence or not.

Eventually the signal came and Kulp swung into action. Each terminal surrounding the unfortunate planet and its black companion was activated, triggering the lethal net which ensnared Moosevan in a web which excluded the normal laws of physics from its interior. The ensuing turmoil of distortion slowly began to twist the peaceful globe out of its natural shape. Every atom it had was rearranged in a different position to the one Nature had put it in.

Soon it was no longer round, but ovate, then cylindrical, then finally spinning like a flat disc. Carefully following Dax's instructions, Kulp held it in that position for the length of time specified, just to make sure nothing could survive. Then he let it snap back into shape with a suddenness that made Tolt, Jannu and the Mott jump.

'It worked . . . it worked . . .' whooped Tolt in relief.

'So it did,' the Mott agreed non-committally, still watching the planet on the monitor. 'I hope this is only a passing effect?' he asked threateningly as he peered at the image.

'What effect?' asked Jannu in bewilderment and scrutinised the image to see what the problem was this time. He did not need to scrutinise it for long; the reality was all too obvious. Instead of the lush fertile world they had promised the Mott for their new outpost, this one looked pretty sick, if not dead.

'What's happened?' asked Tolt in a bewilderment which was becoming part of his reaction to most things.

'If you can't answer that,' snapped the Mott, 'there's no point in asking me.'

'But it should be fertile,' protested Jannu.

'Of course it should still be fertile!' screeched the Mott. 'That was what we paid Kulp so much in advance for. Even the Mott artillery could have laid the planet waste like that without all this paraphernalia. Bombs don't cost a fraction of what Kulp was asking.'

Jannu looked thoughtfully at the derelict smoking heap which had once been a planet, and suggested carefully, 'Perhaps we could come to some arrangement about this?'

'I've already worked out what arrangements I'm going to make,' promised the Mott ominously, 'and after the first few minutes you cease to figure in them at all.'

'Now don't do anything rash,' pleaded Tolt. 'Remember we could stand as witnesses at your trial.' This was a rather pointless appeal as the Mott knew full well he would be dead before the evidence of his court martial was heard.

'Perhaps we could lay our hands on some rapidly evolving plants and things?' Jannu prevaricated.

'So where would you find the atmosphere for them to breathe?' sneered the Mott. 'Shall I lend the planet yours?'

'Oh, I'm sure we could lay our hands on that somewhere as well,' Tolt said evasively. He glanced at the image on the monitor again. 'Look, look . . . the collapsar's gone.'

'Pity,' growled the Mott. 'I was going to shove you two through it. But no matter, you might as well float around in this piece of space for the rest of eternity as anywhere else.'

'Oh you wouldn't,' protested Tolt, knowing quite well they were lucky to be let off that easily.

'I have this terrible phobia about open spaces,' pleaded Jannu. 'You would too if you spent the most impressionable time of your life confined in a jar.'

The way the robots were ignoring Jannu's instructions to stop moving towards them suggested the Mott had taken the precaution of deprogramming the brainwashing he had previously given them. Thankful they were still wearing spacesuits and had helmets to hand, Jannu and Tolt were bundled into the airlock of the Mott station. Hardly had their helmets been clipped tight than they were catapulted into the endless sky with a thousand supernova remnants as a backdrop.

Helplessly they watched Kulp's silent ship hanging some way off, knowing that without the means of locomotion their atmosphere would run out long before chance drifted them together. Even if they had managed to reach it there was no way in for them, and if the planet had been a little nearer, its dead and dingy surface looked far from promising.

'Wonder whether this would have happened if we hadn't

double-crossed Kulp?' Jannu pondered over his communicator to Tolt.

'Of course not. He was going to blast us, remember?'

'Oh yes. Funny how you forget things when everything happens so quickly. I suppose we should count ourselves pretty lucky, considering what the Mott have been known to do to people who'd never even upset them.'

'At least we won't have to worry about having to patronise one of those hideous-smelling deformities again. I suppose Kulp was the best of a bad deal if you look at it from the point of view of ignorant egotism versus egotism of genius.'

'I wonder if there's any life after death?'

'Well,' replied Tolt, 'we'll soon be able to ask Kulp.'

'I always thought he was life after death. At least he was the nearest thing to metamorphosis I ever knew.'

Kulp winced uneasily at that last comment as he listened on his person-to-person receiver. They were not making it easy for him to decide whether to go and pick them up or leave them to follow their orbit around the yellow sun until some more efficient species decided to clean up the littered galaxy.

'Jannu . . .?' asked Tolt thoughtfully.

'What is it?'

'Who was that fluffy creature Kulp got upset with?'

'That was Dax. Surely you've seen a Torran before?'

'Oh yes . . . I've never met one face to face though.'

'You haven't been around much, have you?'

'Making up for it now anyway. What's the chance of finding a surviving robot from one of the beacons and persuading it to take us back to the Mott station?'

'Don't talk rubbish. You don't know when you're well off.'

'Just a thought. My air's getting a bit thin.'

'It will do,' Jannu told him. 'Try not to think about it.'

'Not much else to think about out here, is there? On one side are the dwindling remains of so many sick societies, and on the other the end of the universe.'

'It's no good having profound thoughts now. Anyway . . . you know what happens to philosophers.'

'Something like this, wasn't it?'

Kulp switched the receiver off, unable to stand any more of their banal banter, and turned on the power of his ship. He knew the Mott would notice him as soon as he moved, but as long as he stayed on board his station there was not much he could do about it. He would probably only send out a couple of robots to uphold his honour in combat.

Tolt and Jannu were still engaged in a conversation which grew more and more bizarre as their atmosphere grew thinner and thinner. They were so drowsy they did not notice the hull of Kulp's ship block out the sun's rays. The Mott commander did though. In his mind, the survival of Kulp only confirmed the suspicion he had of them all being engaged in some almighty double-cross. In the one last fling he knew he would have time for before Mott justice caught up with him, he ordered the robots to take the monitoring station out of orbit and line it up to cross the path of Kulp's ship.

'Don't say anything to me until you've breathed enough air to make sense,' Kulp warned Tolt and Jannu, depositing them on the floor of his control room where he could watch them as well as dangers outside.

'I thought you were dead,' Tolt eventually managed to gasp, not willing to admit he was glad to see Kulp again.

'Evidently not. At least I only had to be rescued once. You two actually muffed dying three times. If you weren't so incompetent I wouldn't have bothered to save you, but having two idiots like you around makes me feel secure in my superiority.' He switched his attention to the approaching foe. 'Now shut up while I try to concentrate on what our four-legged friend is up to.'

'When the Mott know they can't colonise the planet creatures' homes,' Jannu whispered to Tolt, 'it's going to upset the plans they had to completely take over the galaxy.'

'Of course it is. What do you think I'm doing here?' snapped Kulp. 'Now shut up!'

Tolt and Jannu looked at each other in mute apprehension. Had their self-centred, egotistical leader noticed the presence of other life-forms in his attempts to swindle, bully and snatch anything he could make a profit out of after all? Had he of all people become a philosopher? Perhaps the shade of pink he had turned to had somehow infiltrated his brain, but the fact that he was still alive must have meant that someone or something had saved him. Even so, gratitude had never been a part of his nature. Before they could silently turn over the possibility of him losing his grip on what he called sanity, an explosion on the hull of the ship told them the Mott had taken things even more badly than they had expected.

'What was that?' yelped Tolt in terror.

'The Mott has diverted the power from his station's engines and is trying to blast us,' replied Kulp.

'But that means he won't survive very long either,' Jannu protested.

'It makes no difference to him,' Kulp explained. 'He needs one last defiant act so it can be recorded he died gloriously . . . even if very expensively, when the station explodes.'

'I rather think we should disappoint him,' Tolt suggested.

'It looks as though we're going to have to,' Kulp agreed. 'If my instruments weren't damaged by that last blast the Mott artillery fleet are on our tails.'

'I don't suppose there's any chance of us going back outside, is there?' inquired Tolt.

'No time to stop, even for that. You're on my side now,' and Kulp pulled his ship out of the Mott's range to swing it in a semi-circle and out of the ill-treated solar system.

Not sure what side Kulp was referring to, Jannu and Tolt decided they preferred the risk of death at his efficient hands, to execution at the incompetent Mott's. They could worry about the dubious condition of Kulp's mental health later.

A deathly hush fell over the gathering of the Mott military high command. Half-seated and half-standing between the two pillars erected to glorious conquest, the supreme commander announced in stentorian tones, 'If anyone so much as mentions the words "evolution" or "genetic engineer" again, they will be taken out of here and blasted.'

At that the silence intensified to the point where the black-striped pillars of conquest might have been heard to whisper, if it had occurred to anyone to listen.

'This should never have happened,' the supreme commander went on. 'That devious miscreant Kulp and his accomplices must have known the vegetation on that planet was dependent on the creature living in it and deliberately misinformed us. Now they will be hunted and done to death.'

At this point murmurs of approval should have echoed through the hall, but everyone was still holding their breath. 'He should have been found out by the commander of the monitoring station, but he too failed in his duty and will be found guilty of incompetence at his court martial. Now we must decide on other strategies to adopt in our conquest of the galaxy. As we are in closed session, this time our plans will not be made public to other species. Whatever we decide will be carried out by Mott engineers for the benefit of the Mott empire.'

As he had warned the assembly to be careful what words it used, none were forthcoming, apart from the fact that no one had wit enough to think of a plan that quickly.

'I will make a proposal, then,' the supreme commander went on, knowing his plan would be accepted and the words he chose to explain it in never challenged. 'We shall construct fleets of bombers that can surround a planet in formation and fire in synchronisation at its surface. This will create complete unco-ordination in their ground and satellite communications, and if we're lucky can exterminate the inhabitants before they can react.'

Though the plan was not all that original it was typical of the Mott, and polite applause rippled through the hall. The supreme commander tucked his other two legs beneath him in his comfortable seat. He knew there would be little problem in extracting the minerals and wealth required for such a project from subject planets. With no one daring to submit a plan better than his, the meeting was dismissed.

Stopping only briefly to gloat over his new plan to tackle old problems, the supreme commander rose and led his entourage back to the discomfort of their grey and black battleship Galacticus 20482201091476.

'Thank goodness that's over,' said one pillar of victory to the other. 'These Mott smell bad enough one at a time, but altogether like that it's unbelievable . . .'

'Can't you stop complaining for one minute?' replied the other pillar. 'The only other alternative was to become one of them.'

'Well, I suppose solid rock does have more charm, but I think I prefer the fur coat again.'

'I'm rather in favour of becoming Kulp now,' was the thoughtful response. 'You can become Tolt and Jannu.'

'Can't you think of anything more aesthetically pleasing than that?'

'It's a good way to lure the Mott. We could lead them into whatever trap we like.'

'Oh, all right. But it's my turn to be Dax after that.'

'Oh, very well. If it'll stop you complaining. But remember we've got only a few million years to clean this place up.'

With a promise to allow Reniola and Dax to use their identities whenever they wished, Kulp, Jannu and Tolt were free to pursue their own brand of havoc-making. The red herrings those two wonder-entities would sprinkle about the galaxy could give them the opportunity for all the engineered mischievousness that had been festering under Kulp's bald pate. He was indeed committed to his new cause, as single-mindedly as he had been to greed. Jannu and Tolt, willing to find out whether compassion had been grafted on to his nature as well, tagged along, knowing there were worse ways of dying than of humiliation.

15

Yuri rolled over and stretched himself drowsily in the soft grass, and opened his eyes to gaze upwards, expecting to see the sky streaked with purple and red. But it was blue and laced with less startling wispy white clouds. Sleepily he raised himself on to an elbow and rubbed his eyes to find he was in the fairy circle below his cottage. The air was warm and he could feel an earthly breeze ruffling his tangled hair.

Wondering if he had dreamt his encounter with Moosevan, Yuri looked about to see if he could find some evidence for her existence. What he saw instead was less reassuring. It was big, bad, black and snorting billows of hot breath on to his face as it glowered down at him with blazing eyes.

'Eva! Eva!' Diana called out as she pursued her friend down the village high street.

Eva turned and looked at her in surprise and concern. 'What on earth's the matter with you?'

'Earth . . . nothing.' Diana giggled with enough hysteria in her voice to make Eva suspicious. 'It's still here, isn't it?'

'Are you having one of your turns?'

'No. No, I've just seen Spalding. He reckons it's all over now.'

'Rather sudden, wasn't it? At least now I know where you've been for part of the day.'

'Where did you think I was?'

'I was looking for you earlier on. I couldn't find Yuri either.'

So much colour left Diana's face that Eva asked, 'You are ill, aren't you?'

'No,' insisted Diana. 'Did you find him?'

'No. Why should you be so concerned?'

Diana shrugged awkwardly, and as the handbag she was holding on her shoulder slid down her arm, it split at the seams and deposited its contents on the pavement. Eva looked at her in bewilderment for a moment, then at the remains of the handbag, and pulled a plastic carrier bag from her pocket to scoop the items into it. Then she came across the reason for the misfortune. It was no larger than a goose's egg, but had the weight of a dozen horseshoes.

'Where did you get this?'

'A friend. It's a touchstone,' Diana said guiltily, trying to snatch it back.

'No chance,' Eva told her. 'You should donate this to science.'

'Meaning you want to chip pieces off it and grind them into powder?'

'Could be difficult with this stuff,' chuckled Eva, as though she was on the track of quark that would solve the riddle of the universe. 'This is something else.'

'It also happens to be mine,' Diana said as she at last managed to seize the rock.

'Where did your friend get it, then?'

'She caught it. I want to find out where Yuri is.'

'Where did she catch it, and why do you want to find Yuri?'

'In a cave, and I want to make sure he's all right.'

'I can see you're going to be a bundle of fun from now on,' Eva sighed. 'I preferred you when you were having hot flushes.'

Diana ignored her. 'Come on,' she said, clutching the rock in one hand and the carrier bag in the other. 'We can take your car.'

'I've got to get some things to the observatory first.'

'Oh, all right. But don't take long.'

Unable to think of any explanation for Diana's fidgety behaviour other than some rogue chemical reaction going on inside her body or, more probably, her head, Eva sped in and out of the observatory as quickly as she could. She was reluctant to leave Diana for long in case she decided to drive off without her; given her jumpy condition the car would not have appreciated the experience.

'Everything all right?' Diana asked as she returned.

'All right?' Eva was bewildered. 'What catastrophic event should I have suddenly discovered to be going on inside the observatory?'

'Everything's all right then.' So, sighing with relief, Diana seemed to relax a little.

Putting Diana's behaviour down to relief at having got through the menopause, but suspecting she had contracted something else in its place which had not yet been diagnosed, Eva drove on. Reluctantly keeping to the ten-mile-an-hour speed limit through the grounds of the museum, she caught sight of the two shaggy museum assistants coming towards them.

'Hello, here comes hair incorporated,' she said.

'Don't be so rude,' scolded Diana. 'You're hardly that immaculate yourself.' As the two young people approached she wound down the window. 'Hello, John. Hello, Fran. Things all right?'

Wondering why Diana kept asking if everything was all right, Eva stopped the car so they could talk.

'Fine,' said John.

'Fine,' said Fran.

'Nothing happened around here for the last few hours has it?'

'No . . .' said John hesitantly, not knowing whether he should be honest or let them find out the unpleasant truth for themselves.

'Well, what happened?' Eva demanded in exasperation.

'You won't like this . . .' Fran began, but did not have the courage to continue.

'I think you should get down to the meadow at the back of your cottage, Di,' John advised her. 'Only whatever you do, don't walk across it.'

Not waiting to ask what they were talking about, Eva started the car and broke the speed limit until they reached the top of the lane that bordered the meadow. There she suddenly braked.

'Go on. Go on,' urged Diana. 'It must have been something pretty appalling for Fran not to have come straight out with it.'

'I can see something else pretty appalling. It's big-bottomed, pompous, and coming up behind us fast.'

'Daphne,' sighed Diana as she heard the hooves of her horse rattling on the gravel. 'Is she trying to catch up with us?'

'Looks like it,' and Eva sprang out of the car like an excited ferret to face her.

'Come back,' protested Diana, more concerned about what was happening on the other side of the hedge. 'Don't start anything, Eva.' But the mounted empress of almost everything she surveyed had arrived.

'Someone of your position speeding, Dr Hopkirk?' Daphne smirked. 'You must have been in a hurry to go somewhere. Don't let me stop you.' Then to Diana, 'I'm so sorry you won't be able to walk across the meadow any more, but it was a waste to let it lie fallow like that.'

'She's set land mines in it, Mog,' declared Eva.

'What's wrong with the meadow?' Diana demanded. 'It'd better not be anything that's going to harm the children.'

'Oh, I am sorry, but it won't be safe for them to play in it any more.'

'What have you done, Daphne?' Diana insisted.

'Why not take a walk down there with me and see?'

'I'll walk behind the horse then,' Eva agreed. 'Some sights are better from the back.'

This was too much for Diana. Without waiting, she started the car and drove off, much to the amazement of Eva, who knew she had never managed to pass a driving test. She turned back to Daphne, and had hardly begun to pass on advice about how to tackle gout and disorders brought on by inbreeding when Diana's voice could be heard calling out, 'Oh my God! Eva . . . Come here this instant!' Eva broke off her conversation and dashed down the slope.

'Oh my God!' she exclaimed. Daphne, smugly convinced she knew what they had seen, let her horse amble down after them. The snippets of conversation that drifted up to her were somewhat puzzling though.

'Oh my goodness, Yuri. What are you doing?'

'Don't pull its tail like that, Kitty. It's very cruel . . . and don't do that, Tom. That isn't very kind either.'

As Daphne reached the bottom of the slope, an amazing sight met her eyes. Yuri had his arm around the neck of the bull and a gin bottle in the other hand, while Vicky was carefully stroking its thick hide. Tom was holding on to an ear while the twins were swinging vigorously on its tail.

'Aren't you ashamed of yourself, Yuri?' Diana was scolding. 'Fancy tormenting the poor animal like that . . . and drinking in front of the children.'

'This bull is my friend,' protested Yuri. 'And when I finish this drink, I drink no more.'

'I'd ask for that in writing if you could hold a pen steady,' grunted Eva. 'And what have you been up to? It looks as though you've wrestled the bull into submission.'

Yuri looked dutifully down at his torn T-shirt and frayed trousers. Without reaching up to his head he knew his matted hair would take a long while to unravel.

'When you've finished playing with your friend, you are going straight into a bath,' ordered Eva. 'And where were you when I called this morning?'

Diana was very interested to hear his reply, though she knew the answer.

'I visit the fairies,' hiccuped Yuri, 'and I play with little big green men who turn pink and all different colours, and talk to furry long-legged thing a hundred thousand million years old.'

'I asked where you'd been' snarled Eva, 'not what your latest delusions were.'

'For him it was probably real,' remarked Diana.

'Like your voices?' retorted Eva.

'What did you call on me this morning for, then?' Yuri asked, altering his grip to hang on to the other ear of the bull for support.

'It doesn't matter.'

'Then it could not have been that important that I was not there,' Yuri told her with blissful indifference.

'He's gone totally mad now,' Eva commented as she watched her husband and the children waltzing the placid bull in circles.

'Perhaps,' replied Diana, 'but what did you want to see him about, anyway? It wasn't anything to do with those exercise books of Yuri's you've got in the back of your car, was it?'

Eva shot her a sideways glance. Diana imagined she could hear the mental snarl which accompanied it.

'Perhaps he was never that mad after all?' Diana suggested gently, and though Eva might have agreed with her, she still said nothing.

Suddenly Yuri caught sight of Daphne astride her mount, wearing an expression of numb astonishment. 'Good afternoon, Mrs Trotter. Thank you for sending little friend for children to play with. He tell us you put him here.'

Diana and Eva did not even bother to turn to see Daphne's enraged expression. Just knowing it was there was enough to satisfy them. They could tell by the swift intake of breath and sudden creak of leather that she was departing. Though the attention of the others was on the playful bull, Diana could not resist looking over her shoulder, and she saw something happen to upset the horse's equilibrium. The tarmac road suddenly pleated and rose up in the air before it. Not used to encountering anything worse than rabbits dashing from under its hooves, this upset the creature. It dug in all four feet simultaneously. As they were going at a good pace, this sudden action sent Daphne sailing over its head towards the ground that had apparently reared up to meet her.

Not wanting to draw attention to Daphne's predicament, Diana turned back to study the antics of the children, young and old, playing in the meadow. She consoled herself with the thought that at least Yuri was obviously happy with Reniola's solution, even if nobody else was ever likely to be.

JOANNA RUSS
THE FEMALE MAN

'A visionary novel about a society where women can do all we now fantasize in closets and kitchens and beds ... intricate, witty, furious ... savage' Marge Piercy

Joanna is from a present time very much like our own, where she struggles to survive and gain acceptance in a man's world; Jeannine, a romantic dreamer in search of the ideal husband, is from an altered past in which Hitler never took power, World War II never happened and the Great Depression continues. Janet comes from the planet Whileaway in the far future, where duels are fought and children born and brought up, but where no men have existed for hundreds of years. All three women are transported from their own times and united by a mysterious figure for an unguessable purpose.

Joanna Russ, Nebula and Hugo award winning author of such remarkable works as *We Who Are About To* and *The Adventures of Alyx*, today remains one of the most important writers ever to emerge from science fiction: she is one of the small number whose work may still be read by those future generations of whom she writes. *The Female Man* is her best known work.

sf

0 7043 3949 8
£1.95

JOANNA RUSS
EXTRA (ORDINARY) PEOPLE

A brand-new collection of fiction and fantasy from one of the most significant writers ever to emerge from the field of science fiction.

The heroic resistance of a mediaeval abbess who resolves to defend her community when a Viking invasion sails up the river ... the adventures of two mysterious passengers aboard a nineteenth century clipper ship bound for America ... a time-travelling heroine disguised as a male God on an errand of mercy in a barbaric past ... a Gothic tale of intrigue and romance between two women.

Joanna Russ once more draws on her talent for vivid characterisation to involve us in worlds not our own, exploring power relationships in past and future to illuminate our own time.

'Souls', the first narrative in *Extra (Ordinary) People*, won a Hugo Award in 1983, *The Science Fiction Chronicle*'s award for the best novella of 1983, and the *Locus* readers' poll for best novella of 1983.

First British publication

sf

0 7043 3940 1
£1.95

SALLY MILLER GEARHART
THE WANDERGROUND

'Machines outside the city, continued Evona, were working no better than usual. Breakdowns were still consistent — planes faltered after less than an hour's flight, trains and autos ground to a stop after short bursts of speed, sails and oars were still the only means of progress over water ... communication with any other surviving city was limited to runners.'

Picture a world where the Earth itself has rebelled against the domination of men — they survive within the cities, but outside them technology, from tractors to guns, fails to operate. But many women have escaped, and within their own communities in the hill country of the Wanderground have developed astonishing physical and mental powers — telepathy, telekinesis, even the power of flight. Now rumours abound that changes within the city may soon affect the lives of the hill women.

The Wanderground provides a Utopian vision of the future that will entertain and exhilarate.

'Sally Gearhart is an original and so is her book. Buy it. Read it. Give it to a friend.' Rita Mae Brown.

First British publication

sf

0 7043 3947 1
£1.95